*The*

# JANITOR

IT'S THE SIMPLE THINGS
IN LIFE THAT MAKE A DIFFERENCE

# GERRY SAVAGE

TREMENDOUS
LEADERSHIP
*Leadership with a kick!*

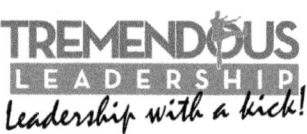

**Tremendous Leadership**

PO Box 267 • Boiling Springs, PA 17007

(717) 701 - 8159 • (800) 233 - 2665 • *www.TremendousLeadership.com*

Tremendous Leadership's titles may be bulk purchased for business or promotional use or for special sales. Please contact Tremendous Leadership for more information.

ISBN-13 978-1-949033-81-6 (book)

ISBN-13 978-1-949033-82-3 (ebook)

DESIGNED & PRINTED IN THE UNITED STATES OF AMERICA

# DEDICATION

For Brady
December 4, 2011 – March 24, 2021

In all my travels past and all my travels yet to come,
I will never find a better friend.

# CONTENTS

# FOREWORD

IT WAS A LATE-IN-LIFE GIFT OF FRIENDSHIP WHEN
my wife connected two Marines who began sharing their time in
the Corps immediately. Of course, places and dates were different,
but our 'Semper Fidelis' experience was emblazoned in our core.

From this unexpected introduction and similar experiences,
Gerry Savage asked if I might write the forward for his book. What
Marine rejects another Marine when they honor him with a personal
request? In addition, I was excited because our professional paths,
beyond our military service, were also similar. In addition to being
Marines, we were both married, raised children, spent a career in
sales, enjoyed sports, and had the love of two brilliant yet down-to-
earth women; not a bad place to start a friendship.

I had read that a good story requires interesting characters,
a plot that holds the reader's interest, a setting that adds texture for
a vibrant context, and tension that needs resolving. So I embarked
on my review with these four elements as my basis for defining a
great read. Barely into my proof copy, Gerry decided to kidnap the
story by inserting a mystery character who just happened to be a
'former" Marine. I was further intrigued as Gerry infused the tale
with salesmanship, serving in the Marines, goal setting, and horse
training. Talk about a rich fabric!

The story is honest and credible, and I was hooked. My new,
talented friend was also a superior 'storyteller,' and the characters and
context came alive. Little life lessons were disguised and engrained

into the plot. In *The Janitor*, Gerry discusses the roles of advocates in our lives used as force multipliers, unpacking who they are, why you need them, and what they can do for you.

And one can't miss that thread of being a Marine and how he sells it throughout his story giving it a sense of place and honor, especially as it earns people's trust. In the end, Ed, the mysterious figure, gives Jack one last bit of wisdom, "Listen to your heart, and your dreams will follow." You'll have to read the book to see how an unexpected ending validates this truth.

More and more life lessons and little tidbits are deposited on your doorstep as you allow Gerry to be both hard-hitting and tender. This book is an engaging read with a lasting impact. I know this is the first of many stories that will come from this author. The future should bring many more insights and lessons, and I eagerly await them.

*Semper Fidelis*

**Michael J. Wheeler**, USMC, Former National Director/ Executive Vice President, First Command Financial Services

# CHAPTER ONE

# INTO THE NIGHT

GOODNIGHT, ELIZABETH. DADDY LOVES YOU. I'LL see you in the morning. Now give the phone back to Mommy."

"What time do you think you'll be home this time?" Mary's voice betrayed her disappointment.

"I'm not sure, honey," I sighed. "I really need to get these month-end numbers done. I'm a little behind, and I just need to get my ducks in a row to justify figures or at least explain why business is coming in as slow as it is."

"This job is going to kill you, you know?" my wife told me more than asked me. "You're going to blink, and Elizabeth will be grown up. Patrick's been walking around the yard with his football all afternoon, hoping you would get home early enough to play pass."

"I know, I know," I could hear the tenseness in my voice as my volume grew louder, cutting the dead quiet in the building.

"Jack," Mary's voice softened, "is everything okay? You seem a little on edge."

"No, no, I'm fine, Mar," I replied without hesitation. "It's the numbers, same ol' thing, just a different day. We are doing everything we can and still sitting at about 89 percent to quota. It's funny . . . but not really . . . the board thinks we should continue to grow 15 percent year over year even though the entire industry is averaging less than half that. Growth is relatively easy when you are new to the market, but as a company matures, hitting that number just gets harder and harder."

"Honey, I know you're doing your best," Mary tried to encourage me. "But, Jack, we need to spend quality time together at the lake. The kids miss you, and I miss you," she sighed. "Just come home as soon as you can."

"I know. I will. I promise," I said as earnestly as I could. "I love you, Mary. I'll try not to wake you when I come in."

Mary was a wonderful wife and an unbelievable mother. When Elizabeth was born just three short years after Patrick, Mary was going to leave her accounting position at the Hudson Group, but the owner didn't want to lose her. Jim Hudson was the third-generation owner of a very family-oriented company. Their expert craftsmen produced top-quality, New England-style furniture from the best hardwood available and distributed it worldwide, including the LL Bean retail store in Maine. Jim arranged it so Mary could work remotely four days a week and only go into the office twice a month.

I often marveled at how she kept it all together. She had her routine, and she stuck with it: quick workout in the morning, getting Patrick and Elizabeth out the door to school, managing her workload, and of course, putting up with me. So, while Mary could hold her own in any executive board room meeting, she preferred the simple life with family. Instead of fighting the crowds and train schedules, she chose jeans, a cozy sweater, and a cup of fresh coffee.

On the other hand, my work had become a never-ending topic of discussion. About a year after Mary transitioned to work from home, I moved into my current role as vice president of sales at US Ortho. When I was promoted, I thought I had finally arrived. But more and more often, I would call Mary and apologize for not being home, then I would hang up the phone and get back to the spreadsheets.

As I hung up the phone tonight, I leaned back in my chair and spun around to look out over the city. The nighttime lighting on our floor had already kicked in, leaving just a dull glow around the perimeter of the engineering and admin area outside my office. I had yet to turn on my desk lamp. I stood and walked to the tall windows. The city lights of Philadelphia seemed to grow brighter as the sky grew darker. A couple of hours ago, people would have been scurrying on the streets 20 floors below, many headed home via the Amtrak or commuter trains at 30th Street Station only a few blocks away.

The lights mesmerized me, and I began to reflect. Here it was, 2018 already. So much has happened in the past 20 years.

I joined the Marine Corps in 1998, just after college. Three years after that, the events of September 11th shook the world, and I found myself right in the middle of the Iraq War and Operation Iraqi Freedom. Again, the Corps toughened me up and instilled the discipline I needed to grow.

Thirteen years ago, I decided to try my hand at sales instead of making the Marine Corps a career. Leaving was a tough decision, but I will forever be a Marine, connected to the Corps like every other Marine who ever served.

US Ortho was smaller when I came aboard. We only had a total hip replacement system and no knee system yet. I had worked hard as a salesman in the field, paying my dues, and then later as a regional manager. It was difficult to recruit good distributors back then, let alone compete. Now, the company was on its way to a large mid-cap, but we still had a ways to go. I glanced at my iWatch: September 20th. It had been almost five years since I became the Vice President of Sales.

My predecessor, Todd Bowman, helped me in a lot of ways. We all need advocates in various areas of our life, and Todd was one of mine. However, Todd was a workaholic. He had been in his late fifties at the time, and he smoked. He also would never pass up a good steak and carried the excess weight to prove it.

Todd's first heart attack wasn't surprising to anyone who knew him well. When he resigned due to his poor health, he recommended me to be his successor. I was always grateful for that. We kept in touch until he passed away last year. He always said he wanted to go out like Bing Crosby, swinging a golf club, and the irony is he did, except he was in Hilton Head and not Spain.

I only wish for him that he had more time. Todd told me in many conversations after he retired that if he knew what life would be like after US Ortho, he would have made better plans. I think he knew his time was limited, and there was a hint of regret in his tone whenever we got on the topics of life and retirement.

While I didn't smoke or drink like Todd, I was still somehow following a similar path. I worked late, chasing numbers, salespeople, and customers all day. It was almost like my old days in the Marines, navigating one landmine after another. Just when I would think we were gaining ground, there would be another fire to put out that would set us back.

Successful in the eyes of many, I made several hundred thousand a year, drove a nice car, and had enough money to do virtually anything I wanted. Yet there I was, another evening tied to my desk, a slave to that success. Those who didn't see the sacrifices couldn't really understand. They would be envious and give anything to be in my shoes. If they only knew.

In the silence of the empty office, I asked myself, *What is success, really?*

Whatever it was, I knew I hadn't achieved it. In the back of my mind, I never considered myself good enough. Maybe that's why I was putting in all the long hours.

This year's bonus would be $60,000 if we could hit 98 percent to quota and more than $100,000 *if* we exceed 100 percent. Early in the year, it seemed very doable. There was a lot of optimism. But as the year wore on, we lost some business, and the new revenue took longer than anticipated to come online. I tried not to think about the money and what we would do with the bonus. My vacations were always to "Someday Island," where I imagined the time-off I would never take and the places I would never go. When we went away, I always felt like I had to be near my phone or computer. It seemed there was always something to chase.

"We can still make it," I said aloud as my mind returned to the present. "Giving up is never an option." *Good thing there isn't anyone else around this late,* I thought, *they would think I was crazy.*

I walked back to my chair and slowly spun it around to face my computer. I just then noticed what sounded like whistling from somewhere in the dimly lit space outside my office when one of the motion sensor lights popped on. I rarely saw anyone else working this late, so I couldn't help but ease out of my chair to investigate.

The executive offices looked the same as usual, but I could still hear someone whistling. The tune sounded like "Danny Boy." I would know it anywhere. My dad loved that song, and he would whistle it often.

Walking around the block of vacated cubicles that took up the space outside my office, I could hear an odd swishing sound. As I rounded the last cubicle, there he was. At first, I saw him from the back, swishing his mop from side to side across the tile floor, whistling as he shuffled forward.

I must have startled him because he took a step to steady himself.

"Excuse me," I said, not even trying to be polite, "who are you?"

He turned to face me and said enthusiastically, "Why, I'm the janitor. Sorry if I bothered you. Was it my whistling? I'll try to keep it down. It just helps me pass the time."

"No, you didn't bother me, but I'm a little confused. In all the years I've worked late, I have never once seen a janitor in here at night. Is this something new?"

"Son, you must really be into your work because I've been doing this floor for the last eight years. I see your office light often, Mr. Kaneen. Your work must be important."

"How do you know my name?" I snapped back quickly.

"You came here just a few weeks after I did. Your office used to be on the other end, but you took over Mr. Bowman's office. It must have been about five years ago now. Mr. Bowman and I used to chat occasionally. I remember putting up the sign for your office the day before you moved from down the hall. I think it was the first week of that January."

"How would you know that?" I asked, still cautious.

"Mr. Kaneen, there is a lot I know, and I guess some that I don't know."

I was more than interested now. The man in front of me stood just a little under six feet tall and had a fairly well-groomed beard and thick, white hair. His bushy white eyebrows gave a softness to his eyes. He wore gray work pants and a gray shirt under black suspenders that traveled up over his broad shoulders. His sleeves were rolled up, and he still had well-defined arm muscles for a man of his age. I could just make out a tattoo peeking out beyond his rolled-up sleeves, the bottom of the eagle, globe, and anchor with the now faded words *Semper Fi*.

Whatever my initial skepticism, I had to give him the benefit of the doubt because he was a brother. "You were in the Corps?" I asked.

"Yep, just like you."

"But how did you know I was in the Corps?"

"I can tell," he said simply. "Besides, someone generally doesn't say 'the Corps' unless they were in too. You know what they say about us, right? 'Once a Marine . . .'"

". . . always a Marine,'" I joined in.

"*Semper Fi*," the janitor said simply.

"*Semper Fi*," I responded.

"When were you in?" I asked.

"Son, I was in the war they called a conflict, Vietnam."

"What years?"

"I was in from '70 to '74. You're probably too young to remember, but we pulled out in '73; it wasn't long after that Saigon fell to the Communists, and South Vietnam surrendered." He sighed, leaning on the end of his mop. "What a waste and a lot of lives lost. Men made the ultimate sacrifice in a war they never really understood. No, it wasn't a conflict—it was a war. And it was a mess."

"Were you drafted?" I asked.

"No, I come from a long line of family that all served at one time or another. I suppose at age 72, most people would be retired, but I don't even like the word retirement. Have you ever heard what the statistics are for people that retire?"

"No, I haven't," I said, adding in partial jest, "but I get the sense you're going to tell me."

"Well, the statistics say most people that retire at 67 only live to 78. So go figure: work for 50 years, look forward to retirement, and enjoy yourself only to die 11 years later. That doesn't seem like a fair trade to me, so I just keep on working."

"It may not be a fair trade, but isn't that what we do in America, at least most Americans? And how can you really enjoy yourself if you are still working at 72?" I asked in bewilderment.

"The difference is, I work if you call this work because I choose to. You see, that's the difference. Most Americans are hamsters on a wheel that goes round and round, but they don't get anywhere. Work is just a means to an end, and, in the end, people don't really want the work or the title or even the money. They want what the money will give them. But money doesn't buy happiness. The only thing money can buy you is financial freedom . . . and it's what you do with the freedom that makes the difference in your life and the lives of the people you touch along the way. It's difficult to get there when you work for someone else. That's the reason people only live 11 years after retirement. They work for someone else all their lives. They try to save, but they generally don't; when they finally get to retirement, they are worn out. But not me. I am not a slave to my work. I do this because I enjoy it, it keeps me fit, it gives me plenty of time to do a lot of other things, and sometimes I get to meet people like you. Work? No, this isn't work, son. I enjoy it."

"Wow! Whatever you're doing must be working," I conceded, "because, I tell you what, you don't look 72."

"I'm flattered," he laughed. "How old did you think I was?"

"I would have guessed 63 or 64."

"Well, thank you, I haven't been carded in years," he winked. "Maybe I look this young because I got off that hamster wheel long ago."

The old man leaned on the end of his mop like a crutch. "The thing about life," he continued, "is that it's too short, and you never get done what you thought you would."

"Yeah, how so?" I asked slightly defensively, thinking I was about to hear a sermon I'd heard a thousand times before.

"I lost many of my friends back in that so-called conflict we talked about, and I can still see their faces and hear their voices and our conversations like it was yesterday. Everyone had all these big plans, But the truth is that you never know when your time's up."

His eyes appeared to glaze, and he seemed to be somewhere else for a moment. He dropped his head slightly as he brought the end of the mop to his chest and began to swish it back and forth again. He cleared his throat to avoid getting choked up. In that moment of quietness and reflection, I could almost feel the honesty in the air.

"Look at you, Jack Kaneen. Here you are in the office at 8:00 p.m. on a Thursday evening, talking to an old fool when you should be home with your beautiful wife and kissing your precious daughter and son goodnight. But no. You're working, son, and for what? Will it matter 20 years from now when your children are grown? Do you remember what it was like when you were young, wondering when your dad would come home so you could tell him about your day? For most of us, our dads never came home early. That's just the way it was."

"I was one of those kids whose dad worked late too, so I know what you're talking about," I hesitated briefly in thought. "But, how did you know I was married and have two kids? Next, you will tell me you're psychic or something?"

"No," he said as his voice faded, "I'm just an old man who sees you repeating a pattern, allowing yourself to fall into the same trap. I saw your family picture on the wall in your office from the doorway. Nice looking wife and kids, by the way. So, take a step back, son. It's Thursday night. Go on home. You are going to blink, your kids are going to be grown up, and you will have missed all the important times—the times when you can watch them play and laugh . . . the simple things. It's the simple things in life that make a difference, make life worth living, make a house a home, and give a man satisfaction. If you don't remember anything else from this conversation, son, remember what I said, 'It's the simple things that make a difference.'"

Just then, I heard my phone ring from a distance, and I quickly raced around the cubicles into my office. But when I picked it up, the person on the other end had already hung up. *Must have been a misdial*, I thought.

"You know, you're pretty insightful . . ." my voice faded as I walked back to where I had been talking with the janitor, but he was gone. I searched the other offices on the floor without a trace. I couldn't even hear the elevator moving.

*I didn't get to say goodbye.*

I walked slowly back into my office and stood in front of the computer, staring at the screen for a minute.

*Maybe he was right*, I thought. *Perhaps I should go home.* I reached down to the keyboard, saved the document, and shut it down.

It was chilly as I walked to the car, and I turned up my collar against the fall breeze, a reminder that winter was just around the corner. As my car warmed up, I sat in the front seat with a blank stare. *Was the old man right? Maybe life is too short.* I put the car into drive and pointed it into the night.

# CHAPTER TWO

~

# A FAMILIAR FACE

I ARRIVED HOME AND FOUND THE BEDROOM LIGHT still on. The garage door opener hummed, and the stairs creaked as usual. I tiptoed all the way to the top and down the hallway.

I opened Patrick's door slightly, and, no surprise, he was sound asleep, clutching his football like a doll. At nine, my son was Tom Brady's biggest fan, or you would think so every Sunday when the Patriots scored. Being from New England, I would always try to find a network carrying the Patriots, so Patrick had grown up being a fan too—like father, like son. Not the most popular team when you lived in the heart of Philadelphia Eagle country!

Six-year-old Elizabeth was sleeping like a princess in her room. Her soft, brunette hair glistened in the glow of the small night light beside her bed to keep away the boogie man. I couldn't help but think back to when she first came home from the hospital. Mary and I would watch her sleep for what seemed like hours.

"Hi, honey," I said softly as I opened our bedroom door. "The kids are sound asleep."

"Well, you're an hour earlier than the last several days," Mary set aside the novel she had been reading. "It's good to have you home. How was your day?"

"Typical," I didn't say that challenges seemed almost insurmountable. "How was *your* day?"

"It was beautiful outside today," she stretched with an extended yawn. "The leaves are starting to change, but it was almost like summer . . . until the sunset, then it got blustery. The kids didn't like it when I said it was time to come in, but the first hot chocolate of the season was enough to entice them."

I laughed, and for a moment, I felt like I was there with them.

I walked into the bathroom for my usual routine of washing up and brushing my teeth, looking forward to climbing under the warm covers and escaping to sleep.

"The kids were asking if we were going to the cabin in Maine next weekend to see the foliage," Mary said as she shifted to look at me.

"I don't know if I can get back from Dallas until late on Thursday night," I said, adjusting the pillow so I could sit up for a while and sliding in next to her. *The drive up north will be brutal*, I thought to myself, *at least 10 hours*.

"Jack, the kids are going to be really disappointed," she added, "and quite frankly, so am I. You told us time and again how you were going to make it different this year, and now we all have our hopes up."

"I know," I replied in defense, "but my distributor in Dallas has an important dinner set up with his key customer on Monday. There will be other meetings the rest of the week."

"Can't you move them just this once? You are missing all the simple things that make a difference."

I must have seemed lost with a blank stare.

"What's wrong?" Mary asked.

"I . . . I . . ." I stammered. "It's just that I heard those same words earlier this evening."

"Really?" she asked. "From whom?"

"I was planning to tell you, but then we started talking about a trip up to the cabin," I paused. "There was no one in the office tonight except me . . ."

"As usual," she nodded.

"Well, tonight, I heard someone whistling. When I walked out, this old man was on the other side of the cubicles mopping the floor. He said he was the janitor. It might not seem strange, except that I have never once seen this man in my office in five years."

"Why is that so strange?" she asked. "You get so involved with your work, I'm not surprised."

"Maybe you're right," I said, "but the guy seemed to know a lot about me. And he said the same thing you just said—almost exactly."

Mary smiled. "Sounds like a wise man to me."

"Maybe so. He was a Marine, so he can't be all that bad." The janitor's advice kept swimming around my brain. "I'll see what I can do about the weekend," I said, and Mary's face brightened. "We can talk about it tomorrow night. I have a meeting in the morning at the office, then I need to go down to Delaware to meet with a doctor, and I'll be back in the office by late tomorrow afternoon."

"Of course, you will," she sighed. Then, after a short pause, she asked, "Jack, are you happy doing what you're doing?"

The question caught me off guard, and I paused.

"I mean, does it *really* make you happy?" Mary emphasized.

"We have everything we want, right?" I answered while I was still processing the question.

"Is that a question?" Mary seemed to be analyzing my response.

"Well, what I mean is, we have a great home and live in a great neighborhood. Anyone in my field would love to have my job." I said, trying to sound as convincing as possible. Maybe I was trying to convince myself. "I'm happy because we have each other and Patrick and Elizabeth. Isn't that what matters?"

"That's part of it, Jack," Mary said carefully, "but there has to be balance. The last five years, it's been all work with you and everything else you just try to fit in. Life can't just be one or the other."

My mind wandered back to my conversation with the janitor. *Maybe I am the hamster on the wheel, running all the time and not getting anywhere. Sure, I have advanced in my career, but maybe all I'm getting here is a fancier hamster wheel chasing a $60,000 bonus like a carrot dangling in front of me for the entire year.*

"Mary," I began after what must have seemed like an eternity, "you're right as usual."

"Jack, it's not a matter of being right," Mary sighed. "We're a team. I think once we get through this year, we need to commit to taking some time to go somewhere to reevaluate what our long-term plan is. I don't care if we ever retire as long as we're happy. I read somewhere that people who retire at 67 only live to about . . ."

"Let me guess," I interrupted, "about 78."

"You read the same article?"

"Nope, but the janitor must have because that's what he said too."

"I like this janitor more all the time," Mary replied as she turned onto her back and adjusted her pillow to lie down. "Just promise," she added softly, "whatever happens the rest of the year, we take the time to talk about the future."

"I promise," I said as I kissed her. With that, we turned out the lights. I adjusted my pillow and, pondering the last few hours' events, drifted off to sleep.

"C'mon," he beckoned, motioning me from the dock while gently setting the rods across the seats in the boat, "we'll miss the best time to fish."

Walking down to the dock, I could see the silhouette of the mountain to the west of the lake. I could just make out clouds in the dim, blue sky as the sun was just beginning to rise, glowing orange over my back to the east. The pond was like glass, not even an inkling of a breeze.

The old man hopped in the boat, settled in, and started the engine as I approached.

"Pull the line and hop in," he said. "I'll take us down to Arnold's Point. I'm glad you decided to take my advice," he said.

"What advice is that?" I replied in a voice just loud enough to be heard over the sound of the Yamaha engine as it whined on down the lake.

"That life is too short: It's the simple things that make a difference. So very few ever get that second chance."

I faced him as we made our way just off the point. His familiar eyes were soft and sincere, and his white beard was long enough to touch the collar of a faded green LL Bean field coat. The motor dropped to almost an idle to begin trolling for togue. That's what we called lake trout up in Maine.

"Let me see your hook," he said as he opened a tin foil wrapper to expose six good-sized smelt. Picking out the biggest one, he sewed it on so it would look just right in the water, like a wounded fish, and then he dropped it over the side for me. "You will get a nice one with that, son; I can feel it. Three colors is all you need. No more than that." He let his line down next on the other side of the boat. The water was so calm that it appeared we were not moving. In fact, everything seemed to stand still, even time.

"These are the times you long for, aren't they?" he asked. "Think about it; most people never get to enjoy it. I bet you're glad now that you got off that hamster wheel. I was worried about you."

I had been staring at the water, admiring the mountain's reflection in the mirror of the glass-like lake. Then, our eyes met as I looked up at the fisherman's weathered face. His voice echoed off the mountain.

"It's the simple things that make a difference . . . it's the simple things that make a difference . . . it's the simple things that make a difference. . . ."

I awoke to Mary shaking my arm.

"Are you okay?" she asked, just as startled as I was. "You were making that sound again like you were trying to say something. Was it a nightmare?"

"No, I don't think so," I mumbled as I struggled to open my eyes. "I was . . . fishing."

"You were fishing?" she sounded confused.

"Yeah, I think I was up at the lake. I was fishing with an old man. I don't know who he was, but I must have known him. His face was familiar, and he spoke as if he had known me all my life."

"Jack, I'm worried about you," Mary said, a concerned look on her sleepy face. "Maybe this is a sign you need to slow down."

It was 5 a.m. No use going back to sleep.

I put the coffee on, let Brady, our Cavalier King Charles Spaniel, outside, and made a power shake with a banana as I did every morning. Then, leaning on the counter, I checked email on my phone and liked a couple of Facebook posts, one from an old high school classmate of a sunrise on the coast in Maine. If the pictures of the Maine coast were any indication, she was enjoying life.

*Enjoying life,* I thought. *What a concept.* I recalled the vividness of my dream, fishing on a brisk morning. *Now that would be part of enjoying life!* I missed the times fishing with my dad when I was younger. I thought we would be doing that same thing when he retired, but he withdrew from everything he enjoyed when he retired, exchanging it for cigarettes and hours in front of the television. The chain-smoking didn't take long to catch up with him, and he passed away at 78 . . . *78, just like the study said.*

Brady was now scratching at the door, not waiting so patiently as he let out a couple of stern barks that said, "Let me in!" Then, he scurried past me to the laundry room as I barely opened the door where his breakfast was waiting. Brady was a typical Cavalier, happy-go-lucky, and everyone's friend.

Sitting on the couch, double-fisting my coffee and shake, I thought about all the follow-up calls I needed to make. It was Friday, and I felt behind as usual. I also had to get that new expense policy finished. When the company was smaller, no proper guidelines were implemented or were loose at best. Knowing I had some experience with that from my past positions, Bill tasked me with putting it together. *Growing pains*, I thought, taking the last sip of my smoothie.

Having wolfed down his breakfast, Brady scampered back into the living room and rolled on the floor, scratching his back, then promptly hopped up on the couch and plopped himself down next to me with his head on my lap. Life was simple for him: I love you, you love me, and that's all that matters. *Wouldn't it be nice if life was just that simple and uncomplicated? It's the simple things that make a difference.* There it was again. I couldn't get it out of my head.

The coffee was good this morning, and as I sat sipping it quietly, I began thinking about my encounter with the janitor the night before, wondering if it was somehow related to my vivid dream. *Who was the man in the boat? Was it the janitor, and why would I be fishing with him? And why did that phrase keep running through my head? It's the simple things that make a difference.* Brady made that very clear. He was now snoring peacefully with the total weight of his head on my lap.

"I'd like to sit here all morning, ol' buddy," I said as I gently lifted his head to the side so I could get up. He didn't move but just kept snoring as I placed a couch pillow under his head to avoid disturbing him. Just then, Mary entered the kitchen and poured a cup of coffee.

"Is there anything I can do for you today?" she asked.

"No, I'm good," I replied. "I just need to get to the office for the morning sales meeting, then it's down to Delaware . . . oh, wait, if you could swing by Lucky Cleaners and pick up my suits. That would be great."

"You do know it's Friday, don't you?"

"Uh, yeah, of course, I do," I answered, wracking my brain for whatever event had obviously slipped my mind.

"Pizza night at Two Brothers?" Mary prompted.

*How* could *I forget?* I shook my head. "Honey, I don't think I'll be home in time."

"Jack," she said with a hint of sarcasm, "we weren't counting on you anyway, but we'll save you a couple pieces of ham and pineapple. Of course, that is if Patrick doesn't get to the pineapples first."

"I'm sorry," I said, pouring my unfinished coffee into a travel mug and then topping it off with some from the pot. Finally, I turned to head out the door, kissed Mary on the cheek, and said, "I'll call you when I get back to the office this afternoon, and I'll try not to stay too late tonight."

"Okay, drive safe and don't speed," she warned. "And don't forget what we talked about last night. It's important."

~

# CHAPTER THREE

# THE PRESSURE'S ON

I T WAS A COOL, BRISK MORNING; TRAFFIC WAS light, and I made good time. I stepped into the elevator with a handful of others. Still, I was alone in my thoughts as I continued to replay my conversation with the janitor and the dream from last night and wondered if they were somehow related. I hardly noticed as we stopped at each floor, and people got off and on. When the door opened to our floor, my mind jolted back to the present and the tasks at hand, another packed day. Walking directly to my office, I placed my canvas bag on the leather chair in the corner and sat at my desk facing my computer like a pilot doing a preflight check.

"Kathy," I said almost simultaneously as I touched the intercom on the phone, "would you be able to bring in the . . ." Before I got to the end of the sentence, Kathy walked into my office with the agenda in her left hand and a cup of coffee in her right.

"Here's the agenda, Jack, and I thought you could use a fresh cup."

Kathy was such a great administrative assistant. After four years, it was like she knew my every move in the office. She took pride in her conservative style, always neat as a pin, and her desk was a testament to her, never anything out of place. She had led her high school swim team to the state championships two years in a row, but you would have to drag it out of her because she never bragged.

Now, in addition to being my admin, she was a wife, a mom, and a part-time coach to her twins, Lindsay and Alexa, as they followed in their mom's footsteps.

"Great coffee, Kathy," I said in between sips.

"Gotta love that Dunkin'," she smiled. "The conference room is all set up. Carol Anderson said she would be here in person because she had some appointments in New York this week, but I haven't seen her yet. Unfortunately, Chris is delayed at O'Hare. Everyone else should be virtual, and I sent the meeting link just a few minutes ago."

"Thanks for being on top of all that, Kathy. I know Bill will want to start right away."

"Actually," she paused in the doorway, "Bill said he is not likely to make this morning's meeting and that he is sure you have it under control."

I shouldn't have been surprised. Bill had been more hands-off than usual lately, except for his preoccupation with our numbers.

"If you ask me," Kathy said over her shoulder as she headed back to her desk, "I think he is busy trying to buy a new car. His desk is covered in car brochures."

That shouldn't have surprised me either, not in the least. I didn't know whether to take his absence from the meeting as a vote of confidence or a sign to be worried. At any rate, I wasn't going to get anxious about it. There was just too much to do and too much on the line.

The conference room was set up, just as Kathy had said, and I took my usual chair, the first to the head's right. When Bill wasn't there, I sometimes sat at the head of the table, although it didn't matter much in these virtual meetings.

Most of my team members came from a sales background and were undoubtedly competent. Still, the closer the company got to that mid-cap status, the harder it was to hit our numbers. I could appreciate the pressure they all faced, even with the advantage of having products in their bags that were unique to our company. I knew because I had been one of them, cut from the same cloth. *Did I have the right people on the bus? Were we going in the right direction?* I knew we did, and I reminded myself that it's all about the vision, the strategy, the tactical plan, and the execution.

I was taking some quick notes when Carol walked in.

"Hi, Jack," she said as she bustled into the room, setting her laptop bag down on the other end of the conference room table on the opposite side.

Carol was a shining star. She had worked in the pharmaceutical industry but quickly grew tired of it. When I interviewed her three years ago, I saw that specific intangible that told me she was driven. Bill hadn't been as optimistic as I was, but she squelched his concern by exceeding quota her first year in the business. Carol was a doer. Driven, she always had goals and well-defined plans to achieve them. She carried herself with a quiet confidence but had little time for idle chatter. Most people had to walk at Carol's pace if they wanted her attention.

However, one of her biggest customers retired this year, and his partner decided to go with another company. Then, through no real fault of her own, she had lost another critical account, Maine Medical Center, because they wanted to cut their number of implant vendors. As a result, Carol only had two out of their six surgeons. Needless to say, she and her surgeons had lost that war, and she was forced to weather the storm of a significant loss in revenue. Not one to be deterred, Carol continued to try angle after angle to get that contract back. She would be the first to tell you that the only way she would fail is if she just stopped moving forward, which in her mind was never an option. I was glad to have Carol on my side. The other managers respected her, and I could see her as a future leader in the organization.

"How was your trip in?" I asked, not yet looking up while I was finishing my notes.

"Uneventful," Carol offered with a tone that indicated it wouldn't have been any other way. "I took the train from New York late last night and stayed at the Courtyard a few blocks away. That makes the trip so easy."

"That's good."

"I had dinner Tuesday with our distributor, Bobby Hart, and one of his docs. And then yesterday, I took the Long Island Railroad to Uniondale to meet with Kyle Banks and Dr. Garner."

"How did that go?" I asked.

"I think it went well. I have a great relationship with Kyle, and Susan Garner is close to coming on board."

"Sounds like a great week!" I encouraged her. "That's exactly what we need."

"Okay," I tapped the Zoom link, "let's get this meeting going."

"Good morning, Jeff," I said as Jeff Price popped up on my screen. He chimed in with his usual, "Howdy."

Jeff had been in the business for over 20 years. He worked with two other companies in management roles as a distributor before landing here. When I arrived, he was already with the company, and it was clear from the beginning that he felt he should have been offered the vice president's position. It took us some time to come to an understanding. Our working relationship had progressed over the last two years, although he still tried to test me when he thought he could get away with it. Jeff had been a soccer player when he was younger and still kept fit into his fifties. He was somewhat of a casual dresser and, even in high-level business meetings, would try to forgo the tie if possible.

Pat Murphy, my fellow Irishman, checked in from Southern California with a simple, "Hey, man." Also in his fifties, Pat was so laid back that nothing seemed to rattle him. He had been a distributor in his past life and was well connected everywhere in the southwest. His distributors enjoyed working with him and were always willing to put their clients before him. But this year had been demanding for Pat. He was diagnosed with prostate cancer in January but has since fully recovered. While not being able to travel had cost him some growth in the first two quarters, Pat seemed to take it in stride. He would tell you, "Hey, I'm just happy to be here."

"How's it going this morning, Pat?" I asked.

"Couldn't be better," he smiled, "warm breeze off the water here in La Jolla and 72 degrees."

Just then, Chris Newcomb's face popped up.

"Chris?" I said in surprise. "I didn't think you were going to be able to jump on."

"Flight was delayed, par for the course," he explained, "but I should be back in Memphis by late afternoon."

"Well, I'm glad you could make it."

Chris was our newest regional manager. He came out of sales operations but had evolved and worked hard to earn the opportunity. He was a quick learner, like a sponge, and once people got to know him, they realized quickly that they could count on him. Chris balanced out the team nicely. He had organization and computer skills that most envied. Everyone wanted to be on his good side because he often bailed them out with spreadsheets and reports that gave them trouble.

Kathy had slipped in and taken the seat across from me with her laptop, ready to take notes.

"Alright, everyone, as you know, this is the last week of the quarter. We are sitting at 89 percent to quota with three months remaining. We will finish the month at just under $50 million. If we continue our current growth trend, we should end at about 92 percent, but that's still short. By my calculations, we need $25 million, or about $8.3 million per month, for the next three months to hit our target. So look at your individual numbers, and let's go around the horn.

"Pat, I know it's been rough for you, but you've exceeded $1.3 million each month this quarter. Getting Dr. Cal Johnson in Texas will give you about 30 more cases right there. I'm going out there to see him for you next week, so we can divide and conquer. I know you have been working on that big group in Phoenix. How close are we there?"

"Well," Pat responded, "the good news is that we just got the approval yesterday. They have already evaluated us, so there won't be any ramp-up. I think both partners are on board, and I should see bookings any day."

"What do you think that will account for?" I asked, twisting the pen in my hand, ready to note the numbers.

"It should be about 15 cases for each, so I'm going to say 25 to 30. So we'll have to see, boss."

"Same with me," Chris broke in. "I have been working on this huge account in Chicago. We have also done the evaluation, and it all hinges on whether or not we can get into the value analysis meeting next week for a final vote. If we do that, I'll not only have free access to bring on Dr. Williams, but I'll have a license to go after his partners too."

"That's good news, Chris. Is there anything we can do to ensure we are on their schedule next week?" I asked.

"Maybe you could call Dr. Williams for me," he suggested. "He really seems to like you."

"Consider it done," I made a note. "What are we looking at for numbers?"

Chris thought about it for a few seconds. "Conservatively about 18 per month through the end of the year, but I'm expecting more going into next year."

"Okay," I wrote down the numbers.

"Jeff!" I exclaimed. "You're at 99 percent to quota! Great job!"

"Yep," he nodded, "just trying to hold serve."

"Carol, what's going on in your region?"

"I'm really close with Dr. Garner. She is interested in helping us with our revision stem next year but said she wanted to get going with the primary. She has had some issues with the other company, and Kyle Banks said she wouldn't have a problem switching to us. Kyle also thinks that if Dr. Garner comes over, her partner will too."

"Okay," I looked over my notes. "When do you expect this to happen, and what does it mean for us?"

"It means about 300 hips, and if we get the knees, it would be another 150, so 450 annually. By November, we should gain another 20 hips per month." Carol continued, "I also got a call yesterday from John French, the head of materials at Maine Medical. He said to stay tuned because they had issues with one of the two suppliers they had contracted. Nothing yet, but that could put us right back where we were before we got ousted."

"Great!" I exclaimed, sitting up straighter in my seat, feeling some excitement building. "How do the numbers look, Kathy?"

"Well," she scanned the numbers she had been adding to the Excel file on her laptop, "if the stars align with all of this, you'll be at 97 to 98 percent to quota. Now, getting one of those big breaks like Carol described might make the difference."

"I think it's amazing that we could even get this close," Jeff offered. "Let's face it, 15 percent growth year over year is an unthinkable ask in today's world."

"And yet this team has delivered it two years in a row," I

countered. "Sure, this is a mountain to climb, but we are all up to the task. The vision of US Ortho is to be the fastest-growing company in orthopedics. And you, this team, are three months away from pulling it off.

"We shared a vision, we developed a strategy, and you guys have executed our tactical plan all year in the face of circumstances outside our sphere of influence. You may be saying we need a lot of luck at this point, but remember this: luck, if that's what you call it, comes because you are good at what you do. Some of you are on track to get individual bonuses. We will be thrilled when we pull out that 98 percent and that company bonus."

"I still contend that they put the quota high so they wouldn't have to pay it out," Jeff smirked.

Before I could respond, Carol jumped in, "Jeff, the fact is that we are trying to get to $75 million on our way to being a large mid-cap company. I know it's high, but, respectfully, at this stage of the game, there is nothing we can do but try to hit the number. If we dwell on what should have been, we will never see what can be. So I'm sorry, but I choose to think about what is possible."

"Well said, Carol," I affirmed her words. "That's the attitude we need on this team."

"I agree," Pat chimed in. "We need to focus on what is possible."

"Remember what Denis Waitley said?" I asked them. "'Through complacency comes the lull of apathy; however, through adversity comes the call to greatness.' We need to look at this quarter as our 'call to greatness,' individually and as a team. So, let's focus on what is possible and go after it."

I paused to let my words sink in, and even Jeff was quiet.

"As I indicated earlier," I picked back up where I left off, "I'm heading to Dallas next week for a few days and hopefully up to

Maine with my family on Thursday. Kathy has been taking notes, but I would like to see an updated breakdown of everything you have in your pipeline—targets, as well as where we are in the process with pricing, approval, value analysis, and trials by next Friday that need to happen. I'm looking for a real gut check on what we can expect in October, November, and December units. Does anyone have any questions?"

It seemed like a full minute, although it was probably just a few seconds.

"Let's do this," Carol said. Pat and Chris repeated her words.

"Yeah, I'm in. Let's do this," Jeff said finally.

"Alright, have a great weekend, everyone, and let's go after this next week!" I added in a positive tone.

Kathy folded her laptop. "That was some great encouragement, Jack," she smiled. "Let me know if you need anything on your way down to Delaware. The girls have a swim meet at 3 p.m., but I'll have my phone."

"In that case, I'll do my best not to bother you. We'll let it wait until Monday unless it's an emergency."

Carol was waiting to talk to me as Kathy left the conference room.

"Thanks for your input, Carol," I said. "You expressed yourself professionally as usual."

"Thank you, Jack," she replied. "I really appreciate that coming from you. I just felt the need to stand up to Jeff's little bit of sarcasm. You've been such a mentor to me, and if there's one thing you have taught me, it's that enthusiasm breeds enthusiasm."

"The challenge for all of us is to channel our energy positively," I added carefully to avoid creating a sense of one team member against another. "You'll find in leadership roles throughout your career that every personality style will challenge you at some point.

We are all different, we all have our own opinions, and we all think we're right," I laughed. "And, let's face it, we wouldn't be an effective team if we were all the same. But, if you think about Jeff, he made his statement on cue today."

"What do you mean?" Carol asked, slightly confused.

"Jeff's region accounts for about 35 percent of sales year to date, and he is 99 percent to quota. If you read between the lines, his comment said, 'They set the quota too high; but look at me, I'm going to make it anyway.' It's his own way of channeling his energy and challenging his fellow team members . . . and maybe drawing a little attention to himself."

"You picked all that up from that one comment?" Carol asked incredulously.

"It's the sense you get when you know your team."

"So he wasn't arguing with you as much as he was actually feeding off your encouragement?"

"Yep, you got it," I grinned. "That's Jeff."

"Well, thanks for the leadership lesson, Jack."

"No worries," I replied, standing to walk Carol to the elevator. "We all have our individual strengths, so we can all help each other."

"I'll keep you posted when I hear something from Maine Medical," she said as the elevator doors slid open.

"Have a safe trip home."

~

# CHAPTER FOUR

# AN OLD FRIEND

THE DRIVE TO DELAWARE GAVE ME TIME TO THINK about the meeting, and I couldn't help but feel we had a shot.

The parking lot at Delaware Orthopedics was full when I pulled in, but I managed to squeeze in when a lady in a Volvo wagon pulled out.

As a sales rep years ago, I was always nervous walking into a doctor's office filled with waiting patients. When I was younger, I was often afraid of my own shadow. Not the case at this stage in my life. I had established relationships and was confident and comfortable in almost any situation professionally.

"Hi, Kristi," I said as I approached the desk. "Dr. Waverly is expecting me."

"He is. He's in his office, but don't keep him too long," she said with a hint of caution. "I don't want him getting behind for the rest of the day." She knew her surgeon only too well. He could be a storyteller at times. "Come on back. I'll buzz you through."

Charles Waverly had been in practice for at least 30 years, and I thought he would have retired two years ago. But, instead, just shy of 68, he was six feet two and broad-shouldered and insisted that he wanted to keep working as long as he was healthy.

"Come in," Chuck motioned as I entered his office. I sat in the chair on the right side of his desk while he finished up a note on the chart in front of him. At that moment, I glanced around the office, observing his certificates on the wall. I think he valued the certificate from his fellowship at the Hospital for Special Surgery (HSS) in New York the most. He referenced it in conversation from time to time, and he seemed to derive an aura of confidence from that experience. Chuck was a thinker, but when he made a decision, he did so with a conviction that led to action.

"Jack, do you feel like you make a difference?" he asked while closing his folder and taking his readers off to focus his attention on me.

"What do you mean?" I asked with a half chuckle, quickly clearing my throat. Chuck could be an imposing presence, and his question caught me off guard.

"I mean, I do hundreds of total joint replacements a year, but I'm at that age where I am wondering if I have made a difference . . . in medicine . . . in the lives of those I love. I don't want to overcomplicate it, but at the end of the day, when I ride off into the sunset, did I waste the time I was given?"

"I guess it depends on what making a difference looks like for you," I began. "I think it's different for everyone, so only you can determine that. And, quite frankly, I haven't determined that for myself."

He turned his chair toward the window and crossed his legs. "You know, if people believe I have done a good job, if my patients can live better lives because I helped them, that's a big part. If my family is proud of what I have done and instilled a good work ethic in my children, I believe my legacy is secure. Still, sometimes I just wonder if I have missed some things."

"It sounds to me like you've covered all the bases."

"No, Jack, I'm afraid I haven't," he continued with a sigh. "I just got back from seeing my daughter in Boston. My grandson is so much like her. I missed so many little things when she was growing up. I can barely remember her at that age." Chuck spun his chair back around. Breaking himself out of his moment of reflection, he folded his hands on his desk. "It's almost like I've overlooked the simple things," he continued. "I think the simple things in life make the difference."

I froze. There was that phrase again!

"Are you alright, Jack?" he asked with a twinge of concern.

"Oh, yeah, I'm fine . . . maybe a little too much coffee on the drive down," I said, trying to cover up my own perplexing thoughts and regain my composure. "None of us is perfect, Chuck, but you have done some amazing work. You still do. I don't think you need a visit from the three ghosts of past, present, and future to determine that."

Chuck laughed. And, just like that, we were back to business.

"So, where are we on the project? Anywhere close to getting the prototypes?" he asked with a hint of hope.

"The engineers showed me some of the drawings," I said in response to his question. "They really liked your design input."

"Jack, aligning a total knee replacement isn't rocket science. Let's face it, kinematic alignment instruments can be great, but half of the designed instruments never get used."

"I think that's where we agree to disagree, Chuck. You don't give yourself enough credit. Doctors who are just getting into this technique will use these instruments. It's only second nature to you because you have done thousands of procedures this way."

"You are too kind, Jack," he smiled, "but I'll take that as a compliment. I wanted to talk this morning because I need to do a series of surgeon-to-patient seminars on the procedure."

"Really?" I asked with a bit of surprise that someone as well-known and well thought of as Dr. Waverly would need to market himself at this stage of his career.

"Don't seem so surprised," he laughed, "an old duffer like me can still reinvent himself. The truth is, I'm part of this big practice now, and I've been losing cases to these guys who are marketing this robotic surgery. You must have noticed my volume drop over the last year?"

"I have . . . but I wasn't going to press you about it. I've done plenty of programs like this, so I'll be happy to help." I pulled out my trusty notepad. "Where were you thinking about doing it?"

"The hospital has a conference center, but another great place would be the community center," he added. "I'd like to plan on doing something once the new instruments are in my hands and working well."

I could sense the enthusiasm in his voice as he began to talk about it in more detail, and within a few minutes, we had a handful of good ideas.

"I know this is below your paygrade, Jack." he said as we both stood up, "but I trust you." He put his arm around my shoulder as we began to walk out together, as we had done a hundred times over the years. "And I know you know what you're doing," he chuckled.

"I'll do some preliminary work and get back to you the week after next."

"You have plans next week?" he asked.

"I have a trip to Dallas . . . but Mary really wants to go to Maine with the kids for a long weekend."

"Are you going?" he asked, raising his eyebrows in anticipation of my answer.

I paused, but before I could say a word, he said in the stern voice of an advisor, "Jack, go, just go. It's a beautiful place. And remember what I said."

"Oh, yeah, I've heard it a dozen times in the last 24 hours: It's the simple things that make the difference."

"Hey, you do listen," he grinned.

Kristi broke in, "Doctor, you have a patient in room one."

"See ya, Doc," I said as I reached for the door to the waiting room.

"Okay, see ya," he said as he buried his head in the chart he had just pulled from a holder on the wall.

"I can't believe you kept him on time!" Kristi called cheerfully.

"He's got a little spring in his step this morning," I replied over my shoulder.

I sat in the car for a minute before I started the engine.

*Chuck was right*, I thought. *The janitor was right. Two old souls.*

I dialed Mary but got her voicemail. "Mar, I just wanted you to know I'm in for the weekend trip to Maine. I'll cut the Texas trip short, and we'll leave Thursday so we get two solid days at the lake. We can talk about it tonight. I'm on my way back to the office, so I'll call you late this afternoon or this evening, depending on how late I work. Oh, and save a slice of pizza for me. Love you. Bye."

No sooner had I merged onto the highway back toward Philly than my phone rang. I assumed it was Mary, but when I glanced at the number on my display, it was Steve Hough. Steve was the most aggressive salesman I knew—he was tenacious, always thinking about how to grow his business. Kindred spirits, we shared a competitive drive that kept us vital in our business. But it wasn't always that way. I had to laugh when I thought about how fiercely we used to compete when we were young sales reps up in Bangor. He liked to tell a story about how we almost got into a fight at St. Joseph's Hospital over an implant we both wanted to show to a doctor. Who would have guessed we would become such good friends? We talked once a month or so about life, business, pretty much anything.

"Hey, Steve! Good to hear from you! I'm on my way back from a meeting in Delaware."

"I'm driving *to* a meeting," he laughed. "I figured the road time would give me time to catch up with you. Are you up to anything other than work?"

"Actually, I'm heading up to Maine next weekend."

"For business?"

"No, with Mary and the kids. We're going to the cabin for a long weekend."

"You're actually going to take some time off?"

"I am," I couldn't help smiling.

"Really?" he replied somewhat skeptically. "I'll believe it when I see the photos on Instagram."

"I know, I know," I said, finding it hard to believe myself.

"What happened to you, Jack? Some visit from Ebenezer Scrooge's three ghosts or something?"

*Hadn't I just said something to Chuck about those ghosts?* "Something like that," I tried to shake off yet another coincidence. "Let's just say my lesson for the week has been "it's the simple things that make the difference."

"Kaneen, you never cease to amaze me!" I heard a ringing over the speaker. "Hey, listen, I'm getting a call from a surgeon I've been trying to connect with for the past week. So let me go, and we'll talk after that trip to Maine. Go have fun, Jack. You deserve it!"

I barely disconnected from Steve's call when my phone rang. Again, hoping it was Mary calling back, I hit the button on my steering wheel to answer the call; but it was Bill Conley's voice on the speaker.

"How did it go with Waverly?" That was Bill, right to the point.

"Chuck is doing well."

"He isn't doing nearly as much as he used to. How old is he anyway?"

"His numbers have dropped a little since he joined the larger practice, but he's not planning to retire soon." I didn't want to say that Chuck was 68 because I knew the path Bill would go down, and I don't think someone is washed up at any age as long as they stay relevant like Chuck was doing. "He wanted to talk with me about a patient seminar to get his volume up. He also just returned from Boston and wondered where we were with his instruments. I'll connect with Chad when I get back to the office."

"Yeah, well, before you talk to Chad, I want you in my office so we can review the month. I looked at the numbers Kathy sent from this morning's meeting. It's looking better, but 15 percent growth and 100 percent to quota is all that resonates with the board. That is unless we deliver more," he added with characteristic sarcasm.

"Will do," I said, pushing the button to end the call.

Our numbers were not where I wanted them to be, not where they needed to be. And while the meeting this morning was positive, it would be a stretch to make it. I needed Chuck to come through with his seminar. We needed Dr. Garner on board. We needed Pat's deal in Arizona and Chris's deal in Chicago. And we needed Maine Medical back. As Kathy said, "if the stars aligned," we might have a chance.

CHAPTER FIVE

~

# THE WEEKEND

B ILL WAS ON THE PHONE, BLUETOOTH IN HIS EAR, putting golf balls when I knocked on the side of the door frame to his office. He motioned me in. Bill could be an imposing figure, standing just over six feet with a slender, well-defined build. He was always working out; at 48, he looked much younger than most men his age. Bill was single, good-looking, with dark hair and blue eyes, but he never seemed to be able to stay in a relationship. Relationships require compromise and a lot of give and take, so no one was ever surprised that Bill could never find the right person. As personality styles go, he was the proverbial "Type A."

"I'll give you $20K and my car, not a penny more," he said in his "confident" voice. Bill prided himself on getting the upper hand, but I got tired of hearing him beat people up on the phone, whether it was a car salesman or not. He knew I was an advocate of the "win-win" approach straight out of Stephen Covey's *The Seven Habits of Highly Effective People. But unfortunately, it* was almost like Bill thought it was a sign of weakness. He seemed to prefer the "win-lose" model: "I win, and you lose."

I sat in the chair opposite his desk and opened my laptop while he finished his negotiation. Bill was a dominator, a driven person, and he wanted you to know it. I learned long ago that to communicate effectively, I had to adapt my conversations to different personality styles.

"Okay, we have a deal," he said, "but I want it ready by tomorrow afternoon, or I'm not taking it." There was a pause. "Great," he said, hanging up the phone and turning his attention to me.

"See, that's how it's done, Kaneen. You have to put people in their place sometimes. Can't let them walk on you."

"Right," I said, intentionally trying to focus my attention on my laptop.

"No, I'm serious," he fired back. "Kaneen, you must be direct with people if you expect to get where I am. It is survival of the fittest."

"I hear you, Bill. I'm glad you got the deal you wanted." I immediately launched into the numbers. "Assuming all goes as expected in the five working days we have left for this month, it looks like we will finish the third quarter at about 92 percent to quota. That's a significant jump from 89 percent last quarter year to date."

"You do know that won't be good enough," Bill said in his "condescending" voice, almost as though he had rehearsed it before I came in. "I want details," he demanded. "Where have we lost business?"

"That's why, as you will see, I laid out the details on the next tab of your Excel sheet. It's not going to be easy, but nothing is. The opportunities are there, and I believe my team will close them. But in answer to your question, we have lost only two surgeons to competitors this year, and that is because their health system pressured them to try the new robot. We also had one surgeon, Dr. Metcalf, retire down in Jacksonville. Pat's business slipped the first few quarters because of his illness, but he is back at full capacity now. Maine Medical went with the two companies that had the majority of their doctors, but Carol just heard that they may not be happy with one of the companies they chose. The rest of it, which again is all laid out in the second tab, is due to a decrease in units overall from current customers."

"Get on it!" Bill retorted quickly, signaling we were done.

When I walked out of my meeting with Bill, the office was beginning to empty for the day. However, I could see that Chad, our head engineer, was still working, his jacket hanging from the corner of his cubicle.

"That you, Jack?" he called.

"Who else would be heading into the office while everyone else is leaving on a Friday afternoon?" I poked my head into Chad's workspace, which was always reasonably neat except for the project board behind his desk, which was filled with his latest ideas and notes. The only one who could ever decipher it was Chad, and it sure made him look like he was related to Einstein. His analyst personality style meant that Chad was an introvert but was always pleasant and engaging. I knew I could count on him when I needed him.

"Hey, I heard you were in Delaware today . . . well, at least it was on your schedule on Google Drive."

"Yeah, I went to see Waverly. He asked how we were doing with his instruments."

"Let me pull the cut guides up for you on Solidworks," he said as I looked over his shoulder. "I think you're really going to like them." Our engineers used Solidworks for design purposes. It was over my head, but I loved to see new designs as they took shape, going from a concept to a 3D model.

"These are really nice, Chad," I said, feeling genuine enthusiasm. "You have done a great job! Why don't you get out of here," I added.

"You know, I think I will," Chad began to shut down his screen.

As I was heading back into my office, I heard him call over his shoulder as he waited for the elevator, "You should take some of your own advice, Jack."

A half-hour later, I sat at my computer, putting the finishing touches on that expense policy. Bill scurried by my office on his way out with his phone glued to his ear while trying to put his left hand through his coat sleeve. I worked for another hour, but just like the computer trying to process and organize the information I was inputting, my brain was trying to process and organize the thoughts running through my head. The silence felt lonely. I shut off my computer, stood up, grabbed my wool topcoat off the rack and my LL Bean briefcase off the chair, and headed to the elevator. Just then, I heard it again—the unmistakable whistle of "Danny Boy." I followed the sound past the elevator down to the other end of the cubicles. Rounding the corner, there he was, mopping away, not paying much attention to anything but his work and his whistling.

"It's you again," I said in a surprised voice.

"I could say the same of you," he quipped playfully.

"Are you going to be working this weekend, Jack?" he asked.

"Actually, I'm going to spend some time with the family," I replied.

"Good for you!"

"Yeah, it seems like your advice is popular everywhere I go."

"Really? What advice would that be?"

"You know, it's the simple things that make a difference," I repeated the words I had heard countless times in the past 24 hours.

"Well, you're a quick study, Jack. I'm glad my words sunk in," he said. "So, what simple things have made that difference?"

I paused for a moment contemplating my answer. "When I left here last night, I peaked in on my kids before I went to bed— so peaceful, so young, and so innocent. I'm missing out on their childhood. Oh, and my wife totally agreed with you when I told her about our conversation."

"Your wife sounds very intuitive," he winked. "She cares about you, Jack. Listen to her. So, what simple things are you going to do this weekend?"

"Well, for starters, morning coffee on the back porch with Mary, Elizabeth's riding lesson, a little pass with a football, a little yard work, with a little jumping in the leaf pile, of course, and maybe some hot chocolate since it's getting cooler in the evenings. And," I added like the whipped cream on that hot chocolate, "we are heading up to Maine next weekend. So I decided to cut my Texas trip short. If I return on Wednesday, we can leave on Thursday and make it a long weekend at the lake."

"How about that!" the janitor exclaimed. "All that from a late evening conversation! You are a man of action when you want to be!"

"My dad used to say, 'Action and inaction are both action, so you might as well take an action that means something.'"

"Your dad was a good man," he said in an almost reflective tone. Then he quickly asked, "So, where is it that you go in Maine?"

"West Carry Pond," I said. "It's east of Sugarloaf and Flagstaff Lake and west of Bingham."

"I know it well," he said, his voice drifting off as he picked up his mop strokes again.

"Oh, you've been in that area?"

"Been? I have fished that area for years," he winked again. "I love Rangeley Lake."

"You fish?" I exclaimed, my mouth hanging open like a lake trout before I mumbled, "of course you do."

"It's a small world, Jack."

"Who knows," I shook my head in disbelief, "maybe we'll run into each other up there one of these days."

"Who knows, Jack? Maybe we will."

"And, if I run into you up there, what do I call you? I mean, what's your name? You obviously know mine, but you never told me yours. Now that we've had two conversations, somehow 'janitor' doesn't seem appropriate."

"Edward," he reached for my hand, "my name's Edward. But you can just call me Ed. That's what my friends call me."

"Well, Ed, I can't seem to shake the coincidences I keep running into since our conversation last night."

"Oh, really? How so?" he prodded.

"Well," I considered how to describe my recent experiences. "You have certainly given me a lot to think about."

"Son, call it wisdom, call it old age, call it whatever you want. Let's just say I have made my share of mistakes, too many to count if I'm being honest."

I didn't say it, but I found it hard to believe that Ed could be anything other than honest.

He paused for a moment and raised his chin off his hand resting on the top of his mop handle.

"I know what it feels like to swim too long in the lake without a life vest. You end up barely being able to tread water. You begin to drown."

"Well, I'm a good swimmer," I played along with his analogy. "You don't need to worry about me."

"Jack, do you ever feel like life weighs you down? Maybe the life vest isn't a great analogy, but I hate to see good people being shackled by the threads in their lives that they have allowed to grow into chains that hold them back."

Just then, the phone in my office rang, again odd for that time of night.

"I'll be right back," I said, leaving my briefcase and coat next to the cubicle as I bounded toward my office.

"Better hurry," he called after me. "You never know. It might be a sale."

Reaching over my desk, I picked up the phone. "Jack Kaneen," I said, but just as I did, the phone clicked.

"Well, it couldn't have been that important," I said as I rounded the far cubicle to finish my conversation with Ed. But just like last night, he was gone. *I guess he had to get to another floor*, I thought as I picked up my briefcase and my coat and headed for the elevator.

SATURDAY morning was the start of a beautiful day, clear and crisp. Fall was definitely in the air. Mary and I shared a pot of coffee. At the same time, the kids played hide and seek—no phones, no tv, just watching them running around, on and off the swings, up and down the slide, hearing the occasional, "Daddy, watch me!"

Patrick and I played pass, and I let him tackle me a dozen times, and Elizabeth even got in on a few of those tackles.

At 10 a.m., Mary called Elizabeth in so she could get ready for her riding lesson. I loved to take Elizabeth to the stables when I could, although, lately, that hadn't been very often. I had grown up riding western, with the occasional urge to ride in an English saddle, mostly because I loved the thrill of jumping. Mary had always ridden English but had given it up after college. With Elizabeth, the apple hadn't fallen too far from the tree. We had started her in lessons when she was three, and she lived for going to the barn on Saturday.

Pennsylvania Equestrian Center was one of the most excellent facilities. The horses were well cared for, which was really important to us. If there was one thing my grandfather taught me, it was our responsibility to care for animals in the best way possible.

When we arrived, Sage was in the paddock on the side of the barn. As we approached, Sage saw Elizabeth and trotted up to the gate, whinnying. He was just as excited to see her as she was to see him.

"I'm coming, boy," Elizabeth called out.

Sage was a nine-year-old bay Quarter Horse gelding with a white snip running the length of his face and four white socks. He was so gentle with Elizabeth that she could quickly put his halter on. In fact, he would even lower his head to help her out. He was just a beautiful horse, and Elizabeth adored him. Actually, it was clear that they loved each other.

Elizabeth's instructor, Alissa Jackson, greeted her in the barn and helped her put Sage in the cross ties so she could groom him and get him tacked up for her lesson.

Alissa was in her early 30s and had been riding competitively since she was Elizabeth's age. Tall and slender, she rode gracefully with quiet confidence. She bonded quickly with her students, and Elizabeth was no exception. Elizabeth looked up to Alissa and listened to everything she said. They had built trust, and Elizabeth was becoming quite the little equestrian.

"When are you going to start riding again, Mr. Kaneen?" Alissa asked as she approached. We watched Elizabeth caringly brush Sage's legs. Alissa knew I had been a big western rider when I was younger, and I could feel her eyes on me as I looked down at the floor and swept my right foot side to side across the dust.

"Oh, I don't know," I said. "I'm just so busy."

Sage automatically picked up each foot as Elizabeth bent down to pick out his hoofs.

"Maybe someday soon," I added.

"You just need to do it," Alissa challenged me. "I don't see how anyone could give up riding once it's in their blood. Besides, I bet Elizabeth would really enjoy riding with her dad."

"You're laying the guilt trip on me, aren't you?" I laughed as I tried to make light of the situation.

"Well, just to let you know, I have a beautiful Quarter Horse mare coming in that you could ride western or English. She'll be here in two weeks. So you should consider her."

"Whoa, whoa," I said in jest. "You should have been in sales! That is quite the pitch."

"Is it working?" Alissa asked, grinning.

"Okay," I couldn't believe I was saying it, "I will give it some thought and talk to Mary about it."

She handed me Elizabeth's saddle, and I gently threw it up on Sage's back, tightening the girth so it wouldn't slip. Elizabeth and I put on his bridle in a team effort, and then I handed the reins off to her.

As I watched her walk off into the arena with Alissa, I was thrilled to see my daughter get such joy out of something I loved.

SUNDAY evening came all too quickly. The kids were tired from the weekend fun and were out by 9 p.m.

"Boy, time flies when you're having fun, for real," I sighed contentedly as Mary and I walked upstairs to the bedroom.

"Jack, I'm so happy to hear you say that," Mary said. Something about her tone just made me feel good. Her sincerity was so genuine.

I started to sit down on the bed but just as quickly hopped back up. "I must get my clothes packed and everything together for Texas. I have an early flight tomorrow."

"What time will you be leaving?" she asked from the bathroom sink where she was getting ready for bed.

"The flight's at 7 a.m., so I must be out the door by 5 a.m. There's hardly any traffic then, so I should be through security by 6 a.m. Gotta love precheck."

Mary was reading when I finally lay down beside her on the bed. "There," I said, "all packed and ready to go."

"What was your favorite part of the weekend?" Mary asked as she set her book face down on her legs.

"The whole weekend was good," I reflected. "Oh, by the way . . ."

"Uh-oh," Mary said in a playfully suspicious tone, "It's an 'oh, by the way.'"

"No, no," I assured her, "it's nothing like that. Alissa Jackson was trying to convince me that we should consider a Quarter Horse mare she has arriving in a couple of weeks."

"What did you tell her?" Mary didn't seem as surprised as I expected.

"I said I would talk to you, and we would give it some thought."

"Well, if it keeps you more grounded and present like you've been this weekend," she barely paused, "then I think we should consider it. Maybe we could even occasionally tear Patrick away from his football to take some lessons."

"Okay. . . well, okay," I replied, giving Mary a kiss and then turning to shut off the light. I pulled the covers tight. Morning would be here in the blink of an eye, and I would return to the grind.

# CHAPTER SIX

~

# TURBULENCE

I WAS STARTLED BY MY ALARM AT 3:45 A.M. IT WAS SO dark and quiet; it felt like the middle of the night. The bathroom was chilly, but the shower water quickly warmed to temperature and felt good. I reflected on the weekend in a daze as the water ran down my face.

Suddenly, like a switch had tripped in my head, my mind pivoted to work and everything I needed to do that day. The dinner meeting when I got to Dallas, the distributor meetings in Austin, there was so much to do if I were going to get back Wednesday evening.

The weekend fading into memory, I quickly got dressed. I kissed Mary on the cheek and pulled her covers up slightly to tuck her in. She barely moved but whispered a faint "love you" as I slowly shut the door. Elizabeth was sleeping like a princess, and Patrick was probably dreaming about being a quarterback for the Patriots. I slowly shut his door and tip-toed down the hallway to the stairs with my shoes in my hand. It was too early to feed Brady, and he barely moved as I picked up my bag and headed for the door. He knew the routine. I whispered, "See you, ol' buddy. Watch the house and take care of everyone." I knew he would, but I just liked saying it because it made me feel good when I had to go somewhere for a few days.

The traffic was light, but the parking garage was already

reaching capacity when I pulled into the B garage. I was lucky to land a decent spot near the exit to the terminal.

There was hardly anyone in the precheck line, and it was a good thing because, while my overnight bag passed through, my green canvas LL Bean briefcase was pulled off the belt to be checked.

"This your bag?" the TSA agent asked, pointing to the table off to the side.

"Yeah, that's mine," I responded with a halfway frustrated tone, yet trying to remain calm and nonchalant about it.

"Okay, let's take a look," the young TSA agent said as she swabbed inside and out for any explosive residue. She then began to look in all the pockets. I had no idea what they saw because it travels with me all the time, but I went with the flow. Just then, she reached in and pulled out a metal knee implant. Wrapped around it was a silver chain with a Saint Christopher medal hanging.

"What's this?" she asked, turning the knee implant in her hand, simultaneously trying to untangle the chain.

"It's a knee implant," I explained, "a sample of the one used to replace someone's knee."

"Huh," she replaced it in the bag and handed me the Saint Christopher medal without saying a word. I didn't say a word either and just slipped it into my pocket.

"Have a great day," she said, passing the bag across the table to me.

"You too," I replied, slinging the briefcase over my shoulder as I walked away toward the gates.

Looking at my watch, I saw that I still had almost an hour before boarding, so I headed up the escalator to the American Airlines Admirals Club and checked in.

"Welcome back, Mr. Kaneen," the man at the desk said with a smile. Obviously, I was a regular. "Do you need any flight information?"

"No, thank you, I should be okay."

"My pleasure," he responded politely. "Help yourself to some fresh coffee."

Fresh coffee. That sounded good. I found a seat near a window and out of the way, set my bags down, and headed straight for the coffee. I couldn't wait to get back to my seat to examine the Saint Christopher medal, feeling inside my pocket to see if it was really there.

When I sat down, I carefully took a sip of my hot coffee and reached into my pocket for the chain.

*Saint Christopher,* I thought, *the patron saint that protects travelers. Well, the timing is good,* I mused. The medal was beautiful sterling silver, just like the chain. *How did it get there? Where did it come from?* I couldn't help but ask myself. I certainly hadn't put it in the bag. I had one when I was younger, but it had long since been lost, and I hadn't seen it in years. Mine had an etch mark on the back and a slight scratch on the lower left side. I held it in the palm of my hand, admiring it for the longest time as I took a few more sips of coffee; then, almost anticipating what I would find, I turned it over. I was speechless. There was no one around to speak with anyway, but I was instantly choked up. I fixated on an etch mark on the lower left side of the pendant. *How . . . how could this be? It couldn't be mine . . . could it?* I thought to myself. I searched my memory for any glimpse of reason, but there was none to be found. I wanted to call Mary immediately, but then she might think I'd lost my mind. Instead, I fell deep into thought, clutching the chain in my hand.

"Now preboarding for American Airlines Flight 639 to Dallas at Gate 62." The announcement startled me. I must have dozed off. Quickly, I gathered up my bags, unplugged my cell phone charger, tucked it in my bag, and headed for the exit.

"See you next time, Mr. Kaneen," the desk attendant said as I hurried past the desk.

"I'm sure I'll be seeing you soon."

The noise level rose as I entered the terminal, and the corridor was crammed with people coming and going to and from flights. Fortunately, my gate was a short walk. When I arrived, first class was just boarding. I scanned my boarding pass on my phone as I walked down the ramp: 2A by the window. I knew the Airbus 320 well, almost like an old friend. I knew what to expect every time. The flight attendant greeted me as soon as I sat down.

"May I take your coat and get a beverage for you?" she asked with a pleasant tone.

"Yes, that would be great, coffee, cream, and no sugar."

"I'll have that for you in just a minute."

"Thank you, I really appreciate it." I never finished the cup in the lounge, so one more for the road, so to speak, wouldn't hurt. I was trying to cut back, but my willpower was weak on mornings like this.

"Here you go, Mr. Kaneen, hot off the press, and be careful. It's really hot. Also, just to let you know, the captain said it may be rough on the climb out and around the storms in the Ohio River Valley area, so we may not be serving breakfast for a while."

"Thanks, Julie," I read her name on the lapel of her uniform as she reached to hand me the coffee. "I'll probably put my headphones on and sleep for a bit once we taxi."

"Sounds like a great plan," she said, turning toward the front of the cabin.

Once first class boarded, the plane filled quickly, section to section by zone. Oddly, the aisle seat next to me remained open through the boarding process, which was strange because the gate agent had already announced it would be a full flight. True to my word, I dozed off. I can sleep anywhere, anytime. I guess that's both good and bad, but in this case, with a short night, the snooze was welcome.

Suddenly, I was awakened by a jolt and shutter.

"Ladies and gentlemen," the voice rang through the intercom, "please return to your seats. I have turned on the 'fasten seatbelt' sign. Unfortunately, we are encountering severe turbulence, more than they told us we would be in for." His voice was calm but deliberate, and I knew this was severe weather. Just then, the plane banked to the right and lost altitude. My stomach felt like I was on the Montezuma's Revenge ride at Knott's Berry Farm in southern California. Gripping my armrest, I suddenly felt petrified, which was unlike me because I had logged so many miles in the air as a passenger and a young private pilot. Somehow, it felt different as a passenger because I felt helpless. As the plane continued its rapid descent and the noise grew louder and louder, a hand grabbed my wrist. I looked to the right, and there sat an elderly gentleman.

The plane seemed to level out just as quickly, and the noise, in comparison, went almost silent.

"Sorry if I startled you," he said as the plane righted itself. "I . . . guess I wasn't ready for that. I don't fly as much anymore."

"Yeah, hell of a way to wake up," I responded.

"I used to fly these things all over the world, first for Uncle Sam but later for Eastern Airlines, which no longer exists. I've never experienced turbulence like that."

"Well, hopefully, we're through that rough patch of weather. I didn't even see you board. I must have fallen asleep."

"Yes, you were out," he smiled. "The flight attendant removed your coffee before we took off so it wouldn't spill."

"How long was I asleep?"

"Well, we've been in the air for about 45 minutes, so I'm guessing about an hour." Heavyset with wavy white hair and a well-groomed, white mustache, the man sitting next to me was one of those people I felt sure I had met somewhere but couldn't place. *I thought to myself that I should be so lucky to have hair like that in my later years.*

"Mr. Kaneen," Julie's voice broke in, "You're awake. Can I get you another coffee?"

"How could I not be awake!" I exclaimed. "I don't think I need any more coffee after that jolt, but a cup of hot tea would be nice and calming."

"And you, sir?" she asked.

"Tea sounds very nice," the gentleman said, "and just a little milk with it if you don't mind."

"I'd like a little milk, too," I added.

"Certainly, coming right up."

"So, you used to be a pilot?" I asked as we waited for our tea. "I started flying when I was 16 but never did much with it and haven't flown in years. I was in the Marine Corps, but I didn't fly. Then work just took over my life."

"So, you're headed to Dallas for work?"

"I am," I confirmed. "I was supposed to be there for the week, but I'm coming back Wednesday to take a long weekend with the family."

"So, you're cutting your business trip short to be with your family, eh?" he asked rhetorically. "Family is important. In fact, that's why I'm on this flight—to spend time with family."

"So, are you retired?"

"I guess you could call it that," he chuckled. "But I think you only 'retire' if you have a job. I love what I do, so I don't ever really plan to retire."

"Interesting," I mused. "I met a guy recently who said the same thing."

"Smart guy," he nudged me with his elbow.

"So, what is this work that you love so much?" I couldn't help but ask. He reminded me so much of Ed that I half expected him to say he was a janitor, so it was little surprise when, after a brief pause, he responded with, "Well, I guess you could say I am in the business of cleaning up messes."

"Here is your tea, gentleman," Julie broke in. "Be careful. They're hot, and I was able to get my hands on one carton of milk if you don't mind sharing it for the tea?"

"Perfect," I said in a satisfied tone as I poured a bit of milk into my tea, watched it swirl, and then handed it to my new friend.

"The only thing missing would be the honey," he suggested.

"My dad liked tea with honey," I reflected, drifting in thought for a moment as the smell of the tea brought me back to the kitchen table at the farm in Skowhegan as a 12-year-old boy. "My grandmother would say, 'You're just like your father. You both have a sweet tooth when it comes to honey.'"

"Nothing like a farm. I grew up on one too. Oh, we didn't have much, but we had each other. And when push came to shove, we all worked together and got things done. Guess that's why I have always thought family is so important."

"Funny, my dad used to say something similar. He said they never complained. They just did whatever had to be done because there was no other option. I think I got my work ethic from my parents and grandparents."

"Your grandparents have left quite a legacy. I can see you were raised right."

"Well, I know they certainly tried. They were part of the 'greatest generation' that Tom Brokaw wrote about in his book back in 2000 or so."

"Well, son, we could all stand to take a few lessons from that generation," he pondered in a reflective tone. "People matter, son. Their stories matter. If the younger generations only knew, if they could walk a mile in our shoes . . . But," he seemed to snap back to the present, "people die, things don't get passed on, and we forget. Before long, there is no one to actually remember. That's one reason books are so important. Some of the greatest self-help and motivational literature came from that generation and earlier: Napoleon Hill's *Think and Grow Rich*, Norman Vincent Peale's *The Power of Positive Thinking*, Og Mandino's *The Greatest Salesman in the World*. Some of their phrases and words are still being used, or more accurately hijacked, by all of the would-be motivational speakers and coaches today. Like Charlie "Tremendous" Jones always said, "You will be the same person you are today five years from now except for the people you meet and the books you read."

"It's the simple things that make a difference," I repeated the words that had now become a mantra.

"I say that all the time," the gentleman exclaimed. "I thought it was all original material," he chuckled at his own little joke. "Can I give you one piece of advice, son?" he asked.

I nodded my consent as I quietly sipped my tea.

"Stay true to who you are and where you came from. Too many people lose themselves. They climb the ladder, but they leave their true selves behind. It's so easy to do in the corporate world. Then people hit midlife and must go 'find themselves' again. They spend the second half of their lives wishing they could go back and change things, but we can never go back. Not that you want to live in the past, mind you. But you always want to take the best parts of who you are and where you came from with you. I'm sorry to get on such a soap box. It's a habit of mine when I see something special in someone."

"Well, I could certainly say the same: there's something special about you."

There was silence for minutes as we sipped our tea together. It was as if we were both reflecting on the conversation and its meaning, yet I couldn't help but think he had delivered a message that was meant for me.

I felt a light pat on my wrist, "If you'll excuse me, son," he sighed, "I may be a few years short of being part of the greatest generation, but this body is old enough that it needs to take a little snooze."

"Not at all," I said. Then, with a last sip of tea, I leaned back and closed my eyes.

"Stay true to yourself, son," he repeated, faintly patting my wrist as we both nodded off to sleep.

"Ladies and gentlemen, the captain has put on the 'fasten seatbelt' sign. Please return to your seats. Start powering down your devices, make sure your seats are in the upright position, and all bags are properly stowed under the seat in front of you. We have started our descent into Dallas and will be on the ground in about 20 minutes," the voice of the flight attendant over the intercom woke me from a sound sleep.

I must really have needed the nap. I noticed that I clutched the Saint Christopher medal in my palm, the chain wrapped around my hand. *I must have reached for it when we were in the turbulence,* I thought to myself.

I turned toward the gentleman in the seat next to me to let him know what a pleasure his company was, but my voice trailed off when I turned to an empty seat. I looked at the restroom occupancy lights in the front and the back of the plane, but they were all green. Just then, Julie walked by, checking tray tables and seat backs.

"Excuse me, Julie, where is the gentleman sitting next to me? The elderly gentleman with the white hair?"

Julie hesitated, a confused and concerned look crossing her face. "Mr. Kaneen, there hasn't been anyone sitting next to you."

"Well, what about the turbulence and the loss of altitude we encountered? He was right here during all of that."

"Mr. Kaneen, we never encountered the turbulence we thought we would. The pilot was able to go around it and choose an altitude that gave us smooth sailing all the way. You have been asleep the whole flight."

"Wow!" I closed my eyes and opened them again slowly. "I must have been exhausted because that was quite a dream."

"I have vivid dreams like that sometimes," Julie patted my shoulder, looking relieved to see me making some sense. "Sometimes I write them down as soon as I awaken because I feel like there's a message somewhere for me."

*I don't have to write anything down,* I thought to myself. I *don't think I'll ever forget that.* I could still feel the pat on my wrist and hear the words, "Stay true to yourself."

The plane touched down uneventfully. I carefully placed the Saint Christopher medal in the inside zip pocket of my LL Bean bag so I wouldn't lose it again. I knew I would always relate it from this day forward to this flight and the conversation I had with a wise old gentleman, if only in a dream.

# CHAPTER SEVEN

~

# THE WINDSHIELD AND THE REARVIEW MIRROR

WHERE TO, SIR?" THE CABBY ASKED.

"The Marriott," I answered, "the one a few blocks from Dealey Plaza. Hang on, I'll get you the address."

"Not necessary, sir. I go there often," he said as he pulled away from the curb. "Unfortunately, it may take longer than usual. There was a bad accident, and I could see the highway going toward the city backed up almost to the airport exit on the way in."

"It's okay," I replied, still a little distracted from the dream on the flight.

"You look like you've seen a ghost," the cabby peered at me through the rearview mirror. "Was it a rough flight?"

"No, apparently it wasn't a rough flight after all," I shook my head. "It was just an early start to the day. I came from Philly, so I was up early."

Sure enough, the traffic was moving slowly just as we entered the freeway. Then we came to a dead stop about a mile into the drive.

"Yep, looks like we're gonna be here a while," he said in a tone that sounded oddly relaxed, considering that the cab business was all about time and money.

"I'm sorry," I said, "I'm sure you're losing a lot of money today."

"I learned a long time ago that money isn't everything," he replied just as calmly. "Besides, one of the reasons I like driving this cab is because I get to talk to people like you. I'm Arty."

"Well, Arty, it's nice to meet you. First, I must say it's a great name, but you don't hear it much anymore. I had a friend growing up named Arty, Arty Porior, but we lost touch years ago."

"It's a hand-me-down," Arty said. "It was my grandfather's name."

"I have my grandfather's name too. It's Jack," I couldn't help but chuckle to myself, wondering about all these commonalities I kept running into.

Now more fully aware of my surroundings, I noticed what a throwback this cab was. It had looked like an old Yellow Cab from the outside, and though the interior couldn't have been cleaner, it had a vintage look. It even had front window wings, those small triangular-shaped windows that you could pop open when you just wanted a little air. Cigarette smokers back in the day loved them so they could flick out their ashes.

"I didn't know they made cabs like this anymore," I commented as I rubbed the vinyl seat covers.

"I like the old look," the cabby remarked, and I realized he was dressed for the part with his flat gray cap. "This cab reminds me of the good ol' days," he added reminiscently.

*The good ol' days,* I thought to myself. *What are the good ol' days?*

"The good ol' days were a simpler time," Arty continued, causing me to wonder if I had actually asked my question out loud. "There was less stress, less multi-tasking," he continued. "It was a time to enjoy life and take in all it had to offer, not the constant treadmill we allow ourselves to get on these days."

"I hear you, Arty."

"You know, Jack, I worked my way up to owning 10 of these cabs."

"That's impressive!" I exclaimed. "It's very competitive out there. You must have worked hard to build your business."

"Hard," Arty shook his head a bit sadly. "Too hard. I wanted what I thought was success, a nice house, cars, a lot of money, but I learned that if that's what you really want, it comes at a high price."

"How so?" I asked.

"You have a family, Jack; any kids?"

"Yeah, I do," I answered quickly. "I've got the greatest wife a guy could ever ask for. She puts up with me, and that's a lot. My son is nine, and my daughter is six."

"I'm about 10 years ahead of you," Arty replied. "I have a son, Arthur, and a daughter, Julia. My wife, Sarah, must know your wife because she is a saint also," he chuckled.

"But, seriously, Jack, when I was struggling to get ahead, I thought I would have arrived when I had all those cabs. But a funny thing happened on the way to that so-called success. I became relentless. I worked hard, that's for sure. The money came, the cars came, and the house came, and I gave Sarah and the kids all kinds of nice things. But it was never enough. When you really think about it, wanting things just to have things is pretty shallow. Still, some people, like yours truly, have to learn the hard way that money and possessions can't buy happiness.

"One day, Sarah hit me square in the face . . . well, not really," he said with a deep chuckle, "but she might as well have. She held a mirror up and forced me to look into it, reflecting on everything happening. I saw that I was just about to lose everything important to me—my family.

"Success at that price wasn't worth it to me anymore. And, to tell you the truth, it wasn't success anyway. It was just all . . . ah, what would you call it?"

"A façade?"

"Exactly!" Arty exclaimed, adding, "nothing but a stage show."

"Wow, Arty, that's deep." I felt like a student of Professor Arty's Captive Cab Classroom. "So, what did you do?"

"I sold my company, all but this cab right here," he patted his dashboard. "And I haven't looked back. Do you know why this rearview mirror I'm looking back at you in is a whole lot smaller than the windshield? It's what's in front of you that's important.

"Life isn't a destination, Jack; it's a journey. So we have to keep moving forward." Arty was on a roll, so I just sat back and listened, taking in every word from the wisest cabby in the world.

"We all make mistakes," he continued. "But we can't let ourselves get stuck in those mistakes like we're stuck in this traffic jam. We have to use our mistakes as lessons to make better lives for ourselves and others. I can never change the past; none of us can, but we can change the future because it hasn't happened yet. There are so many options ahead of us, and we can't let the world tell us which one to take. We can't let other people define success for us. If we do, we'll lose ourselves in the quest to find it. Yes, sir, it's like my dad used to say all the time, 'You have to be true to who you are.'"

The blood must have drained from my face.

"Did I say something to upset you, Jack?" he glanced back at me. "Now you really look like you've seen that ghost."

"No, I'm alright," I shook my head. "I heard those same words from an older gentleman on my flight this morning."

"Well, whoever said it knows it's true," Arty said. I didn't think there was any need to explain that it was apparently all a dream.

"It's just a coincidence, I guess."

"Jack, I don't know that I believe in coincidences. It's just that when we get so caught up in success, we tend to miss the little lessons that are all around us."

Without missing a beat, I said, "Let me guess . . . it's the simple things that make a difference?"

"How did you know that's exactly what I was going to say?" he asked, looking back at me in the mirror like I suddenly had his playbook.

"I met a wise old man a couple of days ago who said the same exact thing, and I've been hearing it over and over again ever since."

"These guys you meet seem to have it figured out."

"They do, indeed. Like you, Arty."

"Well, as I said a few minutes ago, you must stay true to yourself. Don't lose sight of who you are, where you're going, and how you can use the lessons you learn to make a better life for yourself and the people you'll touch."

"Hey, speaking of moving forward, it looks like the road is opening ahead," I pointed out.

"Yeah, the traffic is starting to move. The police must have cleared that accident. We should be at the hotel in about 15 minutes or less. I'm sorry for the delay . . . and all the rambling. I tend to do that now and then."

"No need to apologize, Arty. It wasn't your fault. Besides, this has been the most interesting and worthwhile cab ride ever."

"Why, that's very kind of you to say, Jack. Most customers don't say a word, so I don't either. But I could tell you were different from the moment you sat down in my cab."

"Really? What makes you say that?"

"Well, cabbies know a lot about baggage. Your carry-on bag wasn't all that heavy, but we all carry invisible baggage. Your expression, the way you listened, and how you engaged told me you might be looking for ways to lighten your load. For too many people, their baggage just keeps getting heavier and heavier. Before long, they can barely stand up, much less keep moving forward."

"I get it, Arty," I replied with a calmness in my voice that hadn't been there earlier. "I really think I'm starting to get it."

As the cab made its way through Dealey plaza and down toward the Marriott, I could sense our time together coming to an end.

"Arty," I said, "thank you again for your insight. I know I'm just one of many rides for the day, but I'll remember you."

"Thank you for saying that, Jack. You made my day! And, rest assured, I'll remember you too. Who knows, maybe I'll be your ride back to the airport."

"Arty, the way my last several days have been going, it wouldn't surprise me in the least. Can I have your card?"

I checked into the hotel and headed to my room on the 11th floor. Spending so many nights in hotels gave me a few perks, like staying on the concierge level, where getting to the lounge for breakfast or a glass of wine in the evening was easy.

I called Mary as soon as I got into the room to let her know I had made it safely.

"Give the kids an extra big hug for me, Mar," I said as we ended our conversation.

"I will, honey," she said in a reassuring tone. "And don't worry, Brady will keep your side of the bed warm."

"I'm glad he is your protector when I'm away." Brady was by no means a guard dog, but I always felt a sense of calm knowing he would be watching out for my family. I never told anyone, but if I was honest with myself, I always felt a little empty inside when I was away like I was missing something. *It's the simple things that make a difference.* Finally, I was beginning to believe it.

It was 3 p.m. I had two hours before my dinner meeting with

Andy Dalton, my distributor, and Dr. Johnson. It was just enough time for me to head to the gym and still get cleaned up. When I first started traveling so often, the constant eating out and sitting so much had taken a physical toll on me. So, I learned to force myself to get to the hotel gym whenever possible. As a result, I always felt better afterward, renewed in my body, mind, and spirit.

A little less than an hour later, I opened the door to my room just as my cell phone started to light up.

"Hey, Andy," I answered enthusiastically. "How are you?"

"I'm good," he replied. "How was your flight? Uneventful, I hope."

"No issues," I said, bypassing the topic of my in-flight dream experience. "I like the direct flight."

"Should be a great dinner tonight," he announced with his own sense of excitement. "I'm looking forward to getting some of this business closed."

"Me too, me too," I echoed, stopping short of launching into how we needed it and how I was concerned about the numbers. "Looking forward to it, Andy. See you in about an hour."

"Sounds good. I'll text you when I'm in front of the hotel."

As I hung up, I saw I had a missed call and a message. No surprise, it was Bill. I put it on speaker as I hit play.

"Hey, Jack, calling you from the new ride," he laughed but cleared his throat and got serious. "We're closing in on month end, so I think we should call a sales meeting for Friday to light a fire under everyone for the last quarter. I noticed you blocked yourself as 'away' for Thursday and Friday, but you will have to change that."

I could hear the "no compromise" tone in his voice as I stared out the window, my back turned to the phone on the desk. It was a good thing because I probably would have heaved the phone if I had been holding it. I sat down on the edge of the corner chair, still soaking wet from my time on the treadmill. I rubbed my forehead.

*He can't do this,* I thought. In most companies, 92 percent to quota would be no reason to panic. It wasn't where we wanted to be, but we had the irons in the fire that could get us to at least the mid-90s.

After I blew off the initial steam, I reached for my phone and called Bill back.

"Bill," I said deliberately calmly, "sorry I missed your call. I was on the phone with our distributor."

"Did you listen to my message?"

"Yes, yes, I listened to it." I paused before responding further, but I guess there was a millisecond too much dead space.

"Are you there, Jack?"

"Yes, I'm here," the seconds seemed like an eternity as my mind rewound scenes over the last few days and the words kept ringing in my head. *Be true to yourself. . . . It's the simple things that make a difference. . . .*

"There is no problem here, right?" he said with a degree of assumption and a tone that almost dared me to say "yes."

I cleared my throat. "In my last meeting with the team, I asked for a full update from each manager. Kathy will be consolidating the information." I paused again. "I suggest a Zoom call on Thursday to talk about your expectations. Then, if you feel it's necessary, we can bring everyone in for a live sales meeting next Thursday. That will give them all a chance to make their flight arrangements and pull together PowerPoint presentations for the fourth quarter. As you know, I have plans to drive to Maine on Thursday. I can pull off the road to take the Zoom call on my laptop without a problem, so there is no need for me to change my plans."

"Fine." I couldn't tell whether Bill was using his "confident" or "condescending" voice. "Set the meeting up at the office all day a week from Thursday. But I want the Zoom call this Thursday mid-morning, so we can set the tone for the meeting next week and the deliverables I'll be expecting." Somehow, he made the whole plan sound like it was his idea, but that was nothing new either. Insisting on the Zoom call was his way of feeling like he had won.

"Jack, we also need to discuss your performance," Bill added.

"My performance?" I replied, somewhat confused.

"Yes, I think you are doing too much for your managers. You seem to be doing a lot of hand-holding but not enough holding feet to the fire. I told you when I hired you that it was your job to improve your team, but I don't think they can even manage the basics on an Excel worksheet without you or Kathy cleaning it up. You focus too much on the win-win, but you'll have to get tougher on them."

As usual, Bill didn't bother to say goodbye.

I set the phone down, opened my computer, and sent out the invite for the Zoom meeting at 11 a.m. on Thursday. Then I jumped in the shower. After my flight, my workout, and that phone call, the hot water provided a welcome relief. My mind drifted off as I stood there in the calm of the steamy shower.

*What did I say to Bill?* I felt confident in my decision, but I couldn't help but wonder if I should have told him that I wouldn't give my heart and soul to the company at the expense of my family or if I should have said to him that if he didn't think I was the person for the job that he should just say so. I knew I was good at my job, but I also realized that if I was going to be the very best I could be, I needed to be true to myself. It was just like Arty said . . . or the man on the plane . . . or something Ed would say. *Just wait until I tell Ed about this!*

# CHAPTER EIGHT

~

# GOOD RELATIONSHIPS

B Y THE TIME I GOT DRESSED, IT WAS TIME TO GO.
As I buttoned my cuffs, Andy texted me that he had just pulled up. I texted that I was on my way, grabbed my sport coat, and headed for the elevator.

Typical of a true Texan, Andy picked me up in his four-door F150. It looked newer than I remembered, silver with a charcoal leather interior. When I jumped in, I realized by the dash insignia that Andy had gotten himself a new King Ranch.

"Andy," I exclaimed, "you got a new truck!"

"Good to see you too, Jack," he laughed. "Yeah, I just picked it up last weekend."

"Good for you, Andy! If anyone deserves it, you do."

Andy was six feet two and a lean 185 pounds. He played quarterback at TCU and always looked fit as a fiddle, a feat in itself regarding this business.

"Dr. Johnson is looking forward to seeing you," he said as we pulled away from the hotel.

"That's great," I said. "I am looking forward to talking with him too. By the way, I want you to know that I appreciate you setting up these meetings. It means a lot and shows me just how engaged you are."

"Well, Jack, let's just say it's important to both of us."

"It is, but we can't run an orthopedic business from the office. It's guys like you that make it happen, and it often goes unappreciated."

"Hey, you were in the field, Jack, so you know what it's all about out here. I can't tell you how many corporate guys I blow off because I just wouldn't put them in front of one of my customers, to tell you the truth. But, bottom line, you are in a pretty small club."

"I appreciate that, Andy. It's easy to work with you because you get it."

Before I knew it, we were pulling into the parking lot of Bob's Steak and Chop House. Dr. Johnson had arrived and was at the bar having a drink when we walked in.

Andy tapped Dr. Johnson on the shoulder, and the two men shook hands and exchanged a quick hug. They had worked together for quite a few years, and I could tell they watched out for one another.

"Good to see you again, Jack," the tall Texan said in his baritone drawl.

Dr. Johnson was also tall and slender. *It must be a Texas thing*, I thought.

"It's great to see you again, Dr. Johnson. I've been looking forward to it."

"But, let's not kid ourselves," he said with anticipation, "we all came here for another great evening and a great Texas steak."

"That we did," I agreed.

Before I could ask Andy if he wanted a drink, the hostess was in front of us with menus.

"Can I seat you, gentlemen?" she asked, her voice as sweet as the tea they drink down here.

"Of course, you can," Dr. Johnson replied as he slid effortlessly off his stool, drink in hand.

As we sat down, I motioned to the hostess that I would be the one taking the bill at the end of the evening, which also prompted her to present me with the wine list. I learned a long time ago that in any business dinner, you need to take control of the wine and appetizers quickly; otherwise, you could find yourself looking at a bill at the end of the evening that would be well over the company reimbursement threshold. Of course, Andy and I had been down this road before, so he knew exactly what I was up to.

"You enjoy red with your steak if I remember, right Dr. Johnson?"

"I do, indeed! Any good cabs on that list?"

"Let's see," I said with my voice trailing as I perused the list. "There's a nice California cabernet here that I've had."

"Perfect," he nodded his approval.

Our waitress had arrived, placed a small loaf of sourdough bread in the center of the table, and stood silently for a moment, careful not to interrupt our conversation.

"My name is Leah," she finally said, "and I'll be your server this evening. Have y'all dined with us before?"

"Yes, ma'am," Andy answered for all of us, "but it's been a while."

"Well, welcome back," she smiled. "We have a great bone-in ribeye that everyone seems to love, and it's my personal favorite."

"If it's your favorite," Dr. Johnson chimed in, "then that's what I'll have."

"Me too," Andy agreed. "I love a good ribeye. The bone-in just makes the flavor."

"Well, make that three," I said. "That makes it easy."

"It does," Leah gathered our menus. "I recommend medium rare on these." She was getting no resistance from any of us. "And I'll have that bottle of Cabernet right out for you."

Our conversation moved to business with all the ordering formalities out of the way.

"Dr. Johnson, we have been doing business with you for a while now, and I want you to know that we really appreciate your loyalty. You have people showing you new products all the time, so it means a great deal that you have stuck it out with us."

"It's easy when you get good results, Jack. Your knee works in my hands."

"I'll get right to the point, Dr. Johnson. Your success is why we would like to make your surgery center a surgeon visitation center so new prospective customers can see you in action. You would, of course, be compensated for your time."

"What level of commitment from Dr. Johnson do you think would be necessary?" Andy jumped in, twirling and tapping his spoon methodically on the table. "I mean, what I'm thinking about here is his time commitment." He almost sounded like Dr. Johnson's personal agent for a minute, but it was what he needed to do. Sales is all about relationships; this one was as strong as they came.

"That's a good question, Andy." I launched forward, "I think it will be seamless in the facility, no different than when you bring a new rep in to see Dr. Johnson perform a surgery. It would require conversation before and after the case and dinner the evening before or after to discuss the program and the knee system."

"Dinner? So, we could make this our go-to place, Andy! Looks like we will be regulars here," he said, nodding his appreciation to Leah, who had just filled his wine glass.

"Does that mean you like the idea?" I asked with a slight pause.

"I do like the idea," he said, savoring a sip of his wine and then growing serious for just a minute. "But I'm going to need to run this by the administrator."

"Well," I took a chance based on a hunch, "if you lay it out like a good George Strait song, your administrator will have to check 'yes.'"

"You know George Strait?" his eyes widened.

"Hey now," I chided him, "just because I'm not from Texas doesn't mean I don't know how to ride a horse."

With that, we toasted just in time for the sizzling steaks to arrive.

The dinner was relaxed, and the steaks were out of this world, just as Leah had promised.

We shifted easily to three guys who enjoyed good company, good food, good wine, and honest conversation.

"So, you ride?" Dr. Johnson asked me.

"Well, not so much anymore," I cut another bite of steak, "but I used to when I was younger. My grandfather was quite a horseman, and I was on my way to following in his footsteps when I was younger. I won a championship or two in my teens. I also became much more interested in how horses communicate. I would put my gelding, Chance, in the round pen and watch him go around snorting and bucking. Before long, he would start licking his lips and turning his ear to me, which meant he accepted and trusted me. He would stop and stare at me, and, as I turned away slightly, he would walk over and frequently put his head on my shoulder. When the word started to get out a little, thanks to my grandfather, some local people would bring me a difficult horse to work with. I enjoyed the challenge."

"No kidding?" Dr. Johnson shook his head.

"Dr. Johnson is big into Quarter Horses and barrel racing," Andy explained.

"I take my daughter to her riding lessons when I can," I said. "I sure do love watching her."

"How can you not ride?" Dr. Johnson asked, looking

bewildered. "After hearing your experience when you were younger, it doesn't make sense to me that you could walk away. Once it's in your blood, it's in your blood!"

"Funny, my daughter's trainer, Alissa, said the same thing to me on Saturday. She said she has a mare coming in that I should consider."

"Well, I like Alissa," Dr. Johnson raised his wine glass again. "Things just don't happen randomly, Jack. You should consider it."

"I do miss it, but I have so much to do, you know, like earning a living," I said, trying to joke about it.

"Well, horses don't care if you live in a mansion or a shack," Dr. Johnson winked.

"I haven't really thought about riding for years. My family let the farm go when my grandfather passed away. That was where I learned to ride. But then we started our daughter in lessons two years ago, and, I must admit, it feels wonderful to be back in a stable again. Elizabeth has really seemed to blossom with confidence and a zest for life. Of course, Elizabeth can't see that at her young age, but Mary and I see it taking shape right before our eyes."

"Horses live in the moment and help us do the same. My horses keep me from getting lost in all the minutiae that we humans let bog us down. But you know that Jack, you just seem to have tucked it away somewhere."

"Yeah, my grandfather taught me there is so much more to horses than just getting on and galloping around."

"He was a smart man," Dr. Johnson added. "It's like that with people, too, you know? It's all about developing trust."

"That's pretty deep," Andy commented.

"It is," I agreed. "And I agree with all of it."

"It's not so deep, gentleman," Dr. Johnson said. "It's about being true to yourself, true to what you love, true to what makes you happy. A true relationship with a horse won't let you lose sight of that."

*Be true to yourself!* It seemed like every conversation I had over the last few days was being repeated, each one reinforcing the previous. Like a motion picture with scene after scene, memories that had been buried in a locked vault somewhere in my mind suddenly flashed before my eyes—me walking with the Quarter Horse my grandfather got for me when I was just 13, then fast forwarding to the first time Elizabeth loped off on her own with a massive smile on her face.

"Jack, are you with us?" Andy's voice broke into my reminiscences.

"Oh, yeah," I smiled. "The conversation just brought back some good memories."

"Good enough to get yourself back in the saddle?" Dr. Johnson asked pointedly.

"I think you may have missed your calling as a lobbyist," I laughed. "But, the answer to your question is 'yes.' Yes, I will consider Alissa's offer. It would make Elizabeth very happy, and I know Mary would be in your corner too, Dr. Johnson."

"I knew there was something I liked about you, Jack," he winked, "and your wife sounds like a wonderful person too."

We talked about our families, hobbies, and horses as the evening went on. I was genuinely interested in Andy and Dr. Johnson, not just in the business they could bring in. They reflected the same interest back to me. I knew our relationships were transitioning to friendships beyond superficial pleasantries.

"Well, great wine, great dinner, and great conversation, gentleman," Dr. Johnson echoed my thoughts as he placed his napkin on the table, "but I do have office tomorrow, and I need to get going. Jack, I will get back to you next week about the visitation site. It sounds like something I want to pursue. You and Andy can coordinate a time, and we'll get on a call with our administrator to discuss the details."

"Sounds perfect."

"Oh, and Jack," he added, "I'm going to email you an article you may find interesting. It's on working with horses as partners to develop leadership and team-building skills."

"Equine-assisted learning?"

"You're familiar with it?" he asked in return.

"I wouldn't say I'm knowledgeable, but I've read a little about it."

"This article is by Gerhard Jes Krebs, a gentleman in Germany who developed the program about 20 years ago. I think you'll find it fascinating. I would take my staff if they had a program around here."

"Well, I will certainly look forward to reading it," I said, reaching out my hand to grasp his in a mutually affirming handshake.

As we walked to our cars, I thanked him again. I could tell we were strengthening our relationship, which was a satisfying feeling.

Back in the truck, Andy said, "Jack, that's the first time I have seen Dr. Johnson get that deep on a topic outside of orthopedics. He must think a lot of you. He isn't like that with any of my corporate guys."

"It was a great conversation. It's funny how quickly you can find common ground in a relationship. I think we are alike in many ways, Andy; it's not the business but the fact that we both work hard to find a genuine interest in people."

"I think you can find common ground with anyone if you just relax and listen," Andy added.

"I think you are absolutely right," I nodded as he drove me back to the hotel. "In a previous job, I had a boss who used to say,

'Jack, these people are not our friends.' That never set quite right with me."

"Well, let's face it, Jack, there are always some clients you would never want to hang out with outside of work," Andy laughed.

"True, true," I joined in. "But people like you and Dr. Johnson? Why wouldn't we want to be friends outside of business? Although I know you have to separate work and friendship, you can't expect favors because of a personal relationship."

"That's where integrity comes in," Andy remarked. "I mean, I believe if you're just honest and you do what's right, it all works out."

"And that's why we're friends and not just colleagues."

As we pulled up to the hotel, I shook Andy's hand and stepped out of the F150.

"Always enjoy working with you, Andy. I'll be back in touch next week," I said as I shut the door.

"Safe travels," Andy called out the window as I turned toward the door to the hotel.

It was just a little after 9 p.m., and I didn't have to be up at dawn, so I stopped by the concierge lounge before heading back to my room.

Sipping my Old Fashioned, I reflected on the day.

I enjoyed being with customers like Dr. Johnson and distributors like Andy. Productive meetings made me feel relevant and gave me a sense that I was contributing to something bigger than myself . . . unlike conversations with Bill. But I had to honestly consider what he said about me doing too much hand-holding with my team. My dad always said if you want something done right, do it yourself, but that didn't work well in business. I wanted my team to succeed, but I was never a micromanager. Each member had his or her own strengths, and I always tried to use those best attributes to bring out their best work. Like Dr. Johnson said tonight, it's about building trust. Of course, people sometimes settle for just getting through the next day, the next month, or the next year instead of looking toward the future. Again, one of today's conversations came to my mind. Arty said the windshield is bigger than the rearview mirror for a reason. *How do I keep my team focused on what is in front of us? For that matter, how do I keep myself focused on what is out in front of me? How do I stay true to myself? Definitely food for thought.*

I finished off my drink and headed to my room.

I checked my email quickly and was pleasantly surprised to see a note from Dr. Johnson and the attached article he had mentioned.

*Dear Jack,*

*Always a pleasure to see you. Here is the article we talked about. There is a link in the article to purchase the entire book by Gerhard, which, with the knowledge you already have of horses, would give you all the information and insight into equine-assisted learning you would need to start putting into practice. I hope you enjoy it as much as I did.*

*Talk soon,*
*All the best,*
*Cal Johnson, MD*

Excited about the information and Dr. Johnson seeing me as more than just a corporate guy, I eagerly propped my pillow behind me on the bed, opened the file, and started reading. The article was fascinating. Gerhard described how and why horses are the perfect coaches. As I read on, I couldn't believe how horses, people in general, and the business I was in could be so interconnected.

Then I read this quote: "We go through our lives building outer layers around our true self. We create a mask with all those uncomfortable feelings as we pretend to be someone other than our true selves."

I immediately clicked the link and purchased the digital version of the entire book. The content page showed sections written by 10 licensed practitioners worldwide, including Alyssa Aubrey in the United States. I knew I needed to sleep but was drawn in page after page.

I came across a concentric circle diagram representing the premise behind equine-assisted learning. In the center was a circle with the words, "I am." This circle represents who we are when we are born, our authentic selves. Horses never leave this space, but we humans enter a second outer circle as we age. This larger circle was labeled, "I fear I am." This circle represented all our beliefs and fears linked together to form a barrier to the center of who we indeed are. The final outer circle was labeled "I pretend I am." This last and largest circle represents how we want the world to see us and who we feel we need to be.

I kept reading and reading, but somewhere amidst the pages, I dozed off. Then, the alarm was ringing in my ear in what seemed like the blink of an eye.

I spent Tuesday driving a rental car to Austin, including a stop at the world-renowned Buc-ee's convenience store, which certainly fit the claim that everything is bigger in Texas. My meeting with another potential distributor and his reps went well. Although I didn't close any business, there were some real possibilities to explore.

I rolled back into Dallas late and set my alarm for 3 a.m. It was a routine I had repeated a million times before. Some business travelers spent some leisure time in the cities they visited and then took later flights, but I never did that. With me, it was always business—in and out and on to the next thing.

CHAPTER NINE

~

# DÉJÀ VU

THE ALARM STARTLED ME FROM A DEEP SLEEP. I jumped up, and if the ceiling had been any lower, I think I might have hit it. I showered quickly and was out the door within a half hour.

I had hoped I might see that vintage yellow cab pull up for my ride to the airport, but when I called the number on Arty's card, the dispatcher told me he didn't drive that early in the morning. Imagine my surprise when his cab pulled up at the front of the hotel anyway.

"Arty!" I exclaimed as my suitcase, and I piled in. "I thought you didn't drive this early."

"I was up and heard the call come in," Arty explained. "I knew it was you, so I decided I would grace you with my presence this morning," he chuckled. "Seriously though, sometimes it's hard to get a cab this early, and I really enjoyed our conversation the other day, so I wanted to make sure you got to the airport on time so you could get home to your family. Besides, by the time I get home, everyone will just be getting up at my house."

"Well, it sure is a pleasant surprise," I said, feeling like I had run into an old friend.

"So, how was your trip to our great state?" he asked cheerfully.

"I tell you, it seems like everywhere I go lately, I'm learning something, or perhaps it's an awakening. I really can't explain it."

"Sometimes, Jack, you just need to be open. I call it coming back to the present. Some people call it being mindful. Whatever you call it, something someone says or does jolts your mind, and before you know it, what is hidden in your subconscious begins to surface. You become aware of things you never were before."

"I think I may have to call you Professor Arty. You are incredibly insightful."

"I don't know if I'm insightful, but I can tell you that once you see life clearly, the world's colors seem brighter, and everything becomes more vibrant. Remember what I said the other day?"

"Well, my friend, you packed a lot of truth into that one ride."

"You have to be true to yourself."

"Oh, yes, I remember that particularly," I nodded. "Funny thing is, Arty, I heard that same statement again at dinner that night."

"That's not surprising at all. It's like if I mentioned a yellow cab, you would suddenly start seeing more yellow cars than you ever saw."

Sure enough, I noticed a couple of cabs headed toward the airport. There wasn't much other traffic this early in the morning, which meant that I didn't have to worry about being late for my flight, but it also meant that Arty and I didn't have nearly as much time to talk as we had when we were stuck in traffic. As the cab neared the terminal, I felt like I would be saying goodbye to a dear friend. "Arty, you have been an inspiration to me, and I will never forget you."

"I appreciate it, Jack. We are living proof that it doesn't take long to build a connection."

"No, no, it doesn't," I replied.

"Jack, I'll leave you with this," he said as the cab pulled up to the curb, "being true to yourself will lead you to a brighter future, and, who knows, it could change your destiny."

Knowing I had experienced something I would not soon forget, I slipped my credit card into the slot in front of me as I had before. But this time, the screen went dark.

"This one's on me," Arty said.

"No, Arty," I said, "I don't want you to eat the cost of the early morning fare."

"My cab, my rules," he said with a laugh. "I think we both got a lot out of our rides together. Just pay it forward to someone."

"I will, Arty, I will. Take care, and thanks for everything," I said.

"My pleasure," he said with a grin. And with that, I shut the door and watched him drive away.

I was pleased to find that I had been upgraded again to first class. Same seat as my previous flight. *What are the odds?* I thought.

As I boarded third on the aircraft, I was surprised to see Julie standing there to greet the passengers.

"Good morning, Mr. Kaneen," she chirped. "Nice to have you back with us. I was supposed to be on a later flight, but one of the other attendants needed to switch . . . so here I am."

"Well, it's great to see you again too," I said, placing my small suitcase in the overhead bin and then getting situated in my window seat.

"Can I get you anything?" Julie asked. "Coffee?"

"I think I'll have tea with milk this time," I replied, thinking that maybe the extra coffee on the previous flight had been a little much.

The tea was hot, and the milk and honey tasted soothing. But I stopped in the middle of my second sip when someone sat beside me. My seatmate was an older gentleman, a little heavyset, with white hair and a white mustache.

*Am I dreaming this time,* I couldn't help thinking to myself, *or is this for real?*

"Good morning, sir," Julie greeted him cheerfully, just as she had me. "Can I get you anything?"

"Oh, thank you," he smiled, "I'd say that hot tea right there with a little milk and honey looks perfect."

I felt like I was either on an old episode of *Candid Camera* or *The Twilight Zone*.

"Good morning," the gentleman said, extending his hand toward me. I thought about the hand that had grabbed my wrist during the dream just two days ago. "Have we met before?"

"I . . . I don't think so," I stammered, wondering if he recognized me or was just curious about why I had been staring at him so intently. "But you do look quite familiar."

"Name's Seth," he introduced himself.

"Pleased to meet you, Seth," I recovered my manners. "I'm Jack, Jack Kaneen."

"Kaneen?" Seth shook his head. "That's a name I haven't heard in years. It was actually my grandmother's maiden name."

"Of course, it was," I murmured.

"I beg your pardon?"

"Oh, nothing. Sorry, I just keep running into a lot of coincidences lately."

"Well, Jack, maybe we are related somewhere down the line," Seth smiled. "It's a very old name that originated in Ireland."

"So, you're an Irishman," I stated more than asked.

"Well, lad, now that you mention it," Seth gave me his best Irish brogue, "I do have a wee bit o' Irish in me."

Just then, Julie arrived with Seth's tea.

"Traveling on business?" Seth gestured toward my briefcase as he stirred the milk into his tea.

"I am," I responded. "Although this trip was a bit quicker than usual. I cut it short to take a long weekend with the family."

"You have kids?"

"I do," I said proudly, "Patrick is nine, and Elizabeth is six."
Of course, this wasn't typically information I would give to someone
I had only met a few minutes ago. Still, the odd occurrences I had
experienced over the last few days had me seeing life through a
different lens.

"So, you cut your business trip short to be with your family,
eh?"

*See, there it is! Didn't the gentleman in my dream ask me the exact same
question?*

"But it hasn't always been that way for you, son?" His second
question caught me off guard.

"What would make you say that?"

"Well, for starters, you're in first class, and frequent fliers often
get bumped to first class, so you most likely spend a lot of time in the
air traveling."

"I'll give you that."

"Then, you said you cut your trip short, implying that isn't
always the case. You're still a young man. You have a young family.
My guess is that you are probably hellbent on being successful."

I could have felt offended, but he had a gentle way about him,
and his soft-spoken voice had a soothing quality.

"Don't get me wrong," he added, maybe to soften the blow,
"there's nothing wrong with being successful; you just have to be
careful of the success you seek. It's not just making a lot of money."

"What is it you do?" I asked, hoping he would see that I was
genuinely interested in his answer.

"Oh, I've done a lot of things. Some people would call me a
'Jack' of all trades, but I prefer to think of it as well-rounded," he
said as he patted his hands on his belly. "I was an ironworker at one
time. I built bridges all across the country. Now, I guess you could

say I build bridges between people and between ideas . . . kind of like a counselor."

"That sounds really interesting," I said, inviting him to continue.

"One thing I learned over the years, Jack, is that work is just a means to an end. Ultimately, people don't want the work for the title or money. They want what the money will give them. But money doesn't buy happiness; that's not what I'm talking about. The only thing money can buy you is financial freedom. It's what you do with the freedom that makes the difference in your life and the lives of the people you touch along the way," he paused in his monologue. "True riches lie in giving back, in making a difference in people's lives. But in the corporate world, where people are self-serving, it's easy to forget that God made us in his image to serve others. So, to me, success isn't what you have; it's what you give back."

*Wow, these old guys I keep meeting seem to have it all figured out*, I thought.

"You know, Jack, the fact that you cut your trip short actually says a lot about you."

"How so?"

"Well, for one thing, it says that you are learning some important lessons. Don't you think we should learn something every day, Jack? I know I do, even as old as I am. That's what keeps this old body going."

"Well, I think I have been catching up on some of those lessons the last few days."

"Indeed! So, what have you learned?"

I placed my forefinger and thumb on my cheek, giving Seth my best "deep in thought" look.

"I met a fascinating cabby who reminded me that what's in front of me is much more important than what's in the rearview mirror."

"That's a good one . . . for starters," he grinned beneath his mustache. "What else?"

"The other lesson I kept hearing everywhere I turned was that you must stay true to yourself."

"Another great lesson," Seth nodded. "You know, in staying true to yourself, it's not always the big picture, often it's the little things that make a difference.'"

He no doubt caught the look on my face.

"Something I said?" he asked.

"That's another lesson I've heard at least a dozen times in the last few days," I shook my head incredulously. "How do I keep hearing these words from people I've just met or barely know me?"

"Well, Jack, I tend to think that everything that happens to us has meaning; we just need to be aware enough to recognize it and open enough to accept it."

"I'm beginning to agree with you, Seth."

"Son, that's a lesson I wish I had learned at your age. It would have made some of my decisions much easier over the years."

I wanted to ask him more about his career, the lessons he had learned over the years, and the decisions he had made, the ones he was proud of and the ones he regretted. But, before I could ask him, he said, "I see something special in you . . . just a feeling, but I'm usually right. And you can't argue with an old man; it wouldn't be polite," he chuckled. "Now, if you'll excuse me," he swallowed the last sip of his tea, "I'm going to leave you to ponder our chat while I take a little nap. The Lord knows I need my beauty sleep," he said as he closed his eyes and leaned back.

I gazed out at the white blanket of clouds below. The last few days had been surreal. I had heard it said that we attract what we think about most into our lives. Well, my mind certainly kept returning to the words of the people who had recently touched my life.

I thought I should probably get a little work done, so I reached down to get my laptop from my briefcase. But, before I could open it up, I heard the captain telling us we had about 20 minutes left before arrival. That announcement was followed by the flight attendant's request to begin powering down electronic devices. I couldn't believe I had been lost in thought for nearly half the flight. But the flight attendant didn't have to tell me twice, so I slipped the laptop back into my bag. Then, I found my hand drawn to the inside zip pocket, still holding the Saint Christopher medal. Pulling it out, I had it in my hand and went back to gazing out the window as the plane descended slowly through the clouds.

*Could Seth be right? Could there really be meaning behind all of these messages?* I couldn't help but wonder if God was working with the forces of the universe to tell me something.

We arrived at the gate uneventfully. Seth had awoken right as the landing gear came down. I told him it had been a pleasure to meet him and hoped I would see him again someday.

"You never know when you might see someone again, Jack," he smiled, "or when a word or a phrase comes to mind reminds you of that person like they were right there with you."

"I certainly can't argue with that," I said as I slipped the Saint Christopher medal into my pocket and grabbed the leather straps of my briefcase.

I said goodbye to Julie as we exited the plane, thanking her again for her service.

"Take care, Mr. Kaneen," she replied cheerfully. "I hope to see you again on a future flight."

*Of course, you will,* I thought to myself. *Is there really any doubt at this point?*

Seth and I walked up the jet bridge together like two old friends. As we entered the terminal, we instinctively stopped to shake hands.

"This is where I leave you, Jack," he said as he shook my hand with a firm, steady grasp. "You are a special person. Be open to the lessons around you and take them to heart."

He turned and made his way through the crowd, and I just stood there watching him drift out of sight until he was lost among the travelers making their way to and from flights. I reached into my pocket and pulled out the Saint Christopher medal. I found myself looking in the direction where Seth had vanished and then at the medallion. I was beginning to think there was a reason for everything. As I stood there in the way of the people now cutting around me, I committed to myself to just being open to it.

CHAPTER TEN

~

# REFLECTION

A S I MADE MY WAY FROM THE AIRPORT TO THE city, I began to think about everything I needed to do when I got to the office and everything I needed to get done if I was going to make the long weekend happen. I also began to think about what I would say to Mary about having a conference call on our way up to Maine. I needed to stop putting it off and just call her. Not saying anything until we were on the road would be the worst thing I could do.

"Mary," I said as my Bluetooth connected, "I just wanted to let you know I landed and I'm on my way to the office."

"Ok," she replied. "Glad to know you made it safely. The kids and I can't wait until tomorrow. I have us all packed, except for picking up a few odds and ends at the grocery store, but we can do that in Farmington late tomorrow afternoon."

"Sounds good." I hesitated for just a moment. "Mary, we are still good to go, but Bill insists on having a conference call with the sales team tomorrow in preparation for an in-person meeting he wants to have next week because of quota. We can just stop on the way, though."

There was a pause on her end, and then the silence broke with, "Hey, as long as we have you captive in the car pointing north, then I'll take that compromise."

I couldn't believe her attitude, but it shouldn't have surprised me. Mary always looked for the good in any situation, and it made all the difference, not just for me but for all the lives she touched.

"You're the best," I said with a sigh of relief. "Thanks."

"Why?"

"For putting up with me and this crazy roller coaster ride."

"Well, at least it isn't Montezuma's Revenge," she quipped, referencing the California coaster she knew I never wanted to see again.

I felt less tense after speaking with Mary, but I knew she was putting up with a lot. Nothing was ever consistent, and who knew how she could plan anything with my schedule.

It was early afternoon, but I couldn't resist the urge to stop for a nice cup of Dunkin' coffee. I knew I would be at the office for a while, so the extra kick of caffeine would be welcome.

I made my way to the elevator with coffee in my left hand and my briefcase slung over my right shoulder. As slow as ever, we hit what seemed like every level. Finally, the doors slid open to our floor, and I made a beeline for my office with the mission of not being spotted on the way. Success! Like a stealth fighter, I had made my way underneath the radar.

Sitting down in front of my computer, I pulled out my notepad. Early in my career, I prided myself on committing a lot of information to memory. While impressive when I remembered what I needed to remember, there was no backup. I learned the hard way that, unless I had a system, my day was bound to come crashing down as soon as I forgot to follow up or didn't get back to someone. *Guilty as charged,* I thought to myself. I had tried organizational apps, but I had to admit that I seemed to work better from written notes. I relied on them to get tasks done systematically without bouncing from one job to the next. I had become so much more efficient over the years. It felt good to check items off my list one by one without having to worry about forgetting something. Of course, I might never be as organized as some of my analyst friends. Still, I managed to gain the skills to function effectively in my position. And so, one by one, I began to check off items on my list.

I glanced up and saw some admin folks scurry by my office with briefcases. *Was it that late already?* I thought to myself. Glancing up at the time on my computer, I realized that it was already 5 p.m. So far, I had returned emails, including a follow-up to Andy and Dr. Johnson, a price quote for an account, and a review of our inventory in preparation for an upcoming operations call next week.

I spent the next hour knocking out an agenda for tomorrow's conference call and sent it to the team, copying Bill. Before leaving for the long weekend, I also wanted to draft a preliminary agenda for next Thursday's sales meeting and send it to Bill. He and the board might not share my confidence, but I knew I had a firm grasp on the business and a plan to get us to quota.

I slid my chair back and walked toward the windows to look over the city. The sky was already dark, even though it was only a little after 6 p.m. The days were definitely getting shorter, but the workload never seemed to get any lighter. The bustle of activity beneath the glare of the streetlights nearly hypnotized me. I watched as people raced to get home, just in time to wake up and do it all over again tomorrow. Usually, my work week would be only half over. I slipped my hand into my pocket and felt the Saint Christopher medal. Gently grasping it in my right hand, I lifted it in front of me. I didn't know how or why it had shown up, but it was like I had found a piece of me that had been missing for years. I wondered if maybe Mary had found it and put it in my bag to surprise me. I would have to ask her later. *Although maybe,* I slipped it back into my pocket, *like other events from the past week, it was better left a mystery.*

I returned to my chair and noticed my half-finished coffee sitting by my computer. I didn't need to take another sip to know it was cold. Grabbing the to-go cup, I walked out of my office, heading toward the kitchen to reheat it. A smile came over my face as I heard the now familiar whistle of "Danny Boy."

"Hey, Ed," I called, not wanting to startle him as I walked into the small breakroom.

"Jack!" Ed exclaimed, "I wasn't sure I would see you this week," Ed scooted his mop bucket away from the counter so I could get to the microwave. But just as I reached to open it, my eye caught the basket of Keurig pods . . . Earl Grey tea.

"Would you like some hot tea, Ed?"

"Oh, my break isn't until later," Ed paused, "but I guess I could go ahead and take it now. I sure do like hot tea with milk and honey."

"Why am I not surprised?" I asked, pulling down two mugs from the shelf and popping the first K-cup into the machine.

"So, you've already been to Texas and back?" Ed asked as he propped his mop against the side of the refrigerator.

"I have if you can believe it," I said as I positioned the second cup and breathed in the sweet, earthy smell. "See if there's some milk, will you?"

"Judging from how hard you work," Ed's voice sounded muffled from inside the fridge, "I'm sure you got a whole week's worth of business done." Ed closed the door and held up a carton of milk.

"As a matter of fact, Ed," I said as I pulled out a chair and placed the two steaming cups on the table, "it was one of those productive trips where you get more than you bargained for."

"I do know that kind of trip," Ed said as he sat on the opposite side of the small table. "So, tell me, what did you learn?"

*Learn?* I couldn't help but think about what Seth said on the airplane earlier today about learning something every day. More and more, I was coming to believe that none of these conversations were happening off the cuff. It was as if everything these men said had a reason behind it as if they had no time to waste and were intent on using what they had wisely.

Pouring a splash of milk into my tea, I began, "Do you remember our first conversation, Ed?"

"I do," he responded as he stirred his own tea. "It's hard to believe it was just a week ago because it seems we could have known each other all our lives."

"You remember that you told me that it's the simple things that make the difference?"

"I do."

"And then, within the next 24 hours, I heard that same statement from at least three other people?"

"I recall."

"Well, I repeatedly heard the same message on my trip to Dallas. It just seemed like everywhere I went, I was greeted by someone who had a piece of advice that made sense."

"Jack, when I told you that the simple things make all the difference, what did you find those simple things to be in your life?"

"Well," I pondered for a few seconds before replying, "being with my family, throwing the ball with Pat, taking Elizabeth to her riding lessons, sitting on the back porch with Mary sipping a coffee, and just being together."

"You see, Jack, those weren't activities you had never done before. Too often, in life, business, and in the 'heat of the battle,' we lose sight of what is right in front of us. Those simple things were there for you to see all the time. All I did was prompt you to notice them. You should consider that perhaps you hear the same messages over and over because you have opened your heart and mind to them."

"I'm inclined to think you're right, Ed," I responded. "Sometimes when people, especially people we've just met, start laying their opinions down, our natural reaction, even if we don't verbalize it, is to reject them or their advice. At least that's how I am, but this was different."

"Look at it another way, Jack," Ed suggested, "you obviously came across as someone worth conversing with. Let's face it, we all draw conclusions about people when we meet them, but when we feel comfortable around someone, we just know."

"Well, I certainly feel comfortable with you, even though our first conversation started with me being highly suspicious," I chuckled.

"And see, Jack, I've been here all this time, even though you never noticed."

"I think in sales, sometimes we take our skills of observation and intuition for granted; it seems like I have these past few years anyway. I haven't trusted my gut. But lately, something has been driving me in a different direction."

"What's changing your thought process?" Ed probed deeper.

"I'm not sure, stress maybe, seeing how much my kids and wife miss me, and letting people get inside my head to the point that I forget who I am. That came to a head on the phone the other day when Bill called a conference call when he knew I would be heading up to New England for a long weekend."

"What did you say to that?" Ed asked.

"Well, I wanted to tell him that I have given my heart and soul to this company," I replied.

"Did you say that?"

"No, I didn't," I shook my head. "But I did tell him that we needed to do the in-person meeting next week and that there was no need for me to change my plans."

"That's getting a little bold, isn't it, Jack?"

"Maybe," I set my cup down, "but it's long overdue. Besides, you and more than a few other people have told me recently that simple things make a difference." Of course, I said it in jest, yet I knew Ed could sense I was serious. "The other lesson I kept hearing repeated on my trip that has really resonated with me over the last couple of days is to be true to yourself."

"Well, now, Jack, you've had a lot to think about. I can see that. What does being true to yourself mean to you?"

"I'm not entirely sure," I hadn't really put these thoughts into words yet, "but I think it has much to do with being honest with yourself. I think it means not losing sight of who you are and staying true to your values and what's important to you."

"That's a good start. But, when you consider the question, 'Am I being true to myself?' it begs the question, 'Who am I really?' You see, we wear masks that are nothing more than how we want to be viewed by the world. But, the farther we get away from our true selves, the more we secure a future that is less than we are capable of being."

"Are you saying I'm not living up to my potential?"

"No, no, not at all, Jack," Ed reassured me. "What I'm saying is that life isn't just existence. It's also being aware and present enough to discover what you were put here to do; you can't do that to your full extent unless you get back to who you really are inside." He leaned forward, propping on his elbows and looking at me intently. "Jack, I believe we are born with God-given intuition. But as life unfolds, we get exposed to the environment we live in and the people around us. As we try to become what situations demand of us, who the people around us expect us to be, we bury our true selves under years of 'do this' and 'don't do that.' Don't get me wrong, I'm not saying this is all bad. I'm saying that eventually, we learn to survive in this world by putting on masks to cover who we know ourselves to be. Then the longer we wear those masks, the more we confuse them with who we are at our core, often at the sacrifice of our full potential."

"I have been reading a book about working with horses that talks about that concept. The author uses a diagram of concentric circles to help you visualize it. He labeled the small circle in the center "I am;" the next larger circle he labeled "I fear I am," and he labeled the largest outer circle "I pretend I am." That outer circle would be where we develop and wear those masks."

"That's a great illustration, Jack. We create that outer ring to protect ourselves from the world, but it also blocks us from being able to get back to who we were really born to be."

"That's exactly what the author of this book said."

"I like to think of the past as a book, a textbook. You can go back and reread it at any time. The present, well, that's what you learned from that textbook. And the future? Well, now, that's filled with possibilities."

"That reminds me of something a cabby I met in Dallas said to me. He said that the rearview mirror is a whole lot smaller than the windshield because it's what's in front of you that's most important."

"Those cabbies can be such philosophers," Ed said with what seemed to be a somewhat mischievous look in his eye. "You gotta figure they spend much time looking in the rearview mirror speaking to customers. They know it's what's ahead that's most important in life. The trick is not thinking of your past as events that you can categorize as good or bad. When I said the past is like a textbook, I meant that you can learn from it just like a textbook. If you are a dedicated student and learn your lessons well, then the past does not have to repeat itself. But that doesn't mean you are bound to every lesson plan in it."

"But you said that this 'textbook' is our past. You can't just wipe away the past. Everything we have done in our lives; it's all there, tucked away in memory forever. Doesn't everything in our past affect our future and who we are even now?"

"Sure it does, but you can change anything from that book anytime."

"Oh, really," I replied with healthy skepticism, "and how is that?"

"You decide, Jack. You just decide to change your direction," Ed said with conviction. "Your recent decisions may not change your past, but they can certainly change how that past plays out in your future. But, of course, then you have to follow through on your decisions."

"Wow, Ed, you are quite the philosopher yourself."

"I'm no more or less wise than you will be at my age, Jack. It's just that I've been around long enough to make many mistakes and live to talk about them."

"I don't know what I'm searching for," I stood up to take my cup to the sink and wash it out.

"What I am saying is that you have begun a search. I don't know what you will find, but I can see you are searching, and the fact that you are puts you that much farther ahead than others who never ask the questions."

"A lot of what you are saying is starting to make sense, especially after these last few days. I'll have plenty of time to think about it in the car tomorrow and in Maine over the next few days."

"That's right! You decided to go to Maine," Ed exclaimed. "Good for you, Jack! You're on the path to discovering who you really are."

"Ed, I really appreciate this conversation tonight," I reached out to shake his hand. "If I don't see you for a while, have a great rest of your week and weekend."

"Thanks, Jack," Ed replied with a grin and firm grip. "Safe travels, and enjoy the time with that beautiful family."

# CHAPTER ELEVEN

~

# THE JOURNEY NORTH

MARY HAD EVERYTHING STAGED BY THE DOOR when I got home. Not only that, but the comforting aroma of apple pie in the oven greeted me. Brady greeted me, too, his tail wagging with excitement as he paced back and forth because he knew exactly where we were going.

"Don't even think about a piece of pie," Mary said before I could ask. "They're for the trip." But after a long face with a bit of acting on my part, she revealed a perfect apple turnover. Mary knew they were my favorite and just right with a cup of tea.

"Annie called and said she would meet us at the cabin for the weekend. I think she wants to talk to us about something, but she said it could wait and that she is looking forward to big hugs from everyone."

Annie was my big sister, and, like a big sister, she was always looking out for me, even when I insisted I didn't need any help. Even though she was only three years older than me, Annie had greater wisdom than most. She and Mary had become close over the years, and while they wouldn't call it ganging up on me, they made an excellent team to look out for me.

"That's great! I'm glad she can make it." The thought of us being together, even just for a few days, brought back good memories and warm feelings of time spent with family that I was missing in the everyday pace of life.

As we climbed into bed, Mary wanted to hear about the Dallas trip. I explained that I had made good progress with Dr. Johnson, opened a few doors for some much-needed new business, and, just as importantly, met some interesting people and made some new friends.

"Why is Bill calling a conference call when he knows you will be driving all day tomorrow?" Mary asked, and I could tell by her tone that she was trying to hide her disappointment.

"It's Bill," I replied. "He thinks that if he sticks his nose in, the business will just appear somehow. It's his way of feeling like a leader; or, who knows, maybe he is just justifying his existence."

"Jack, be nice," Mary chided as she reached for her book on the nightstand. "I'm sure he is under a lot of pressure too." Always the one to look for a bright spot in an otherwise less-than-perfect situation, Mary often helped me reframe my perspective, reassuring me that circumstances were rarely as dire as they might seem. "So, what time is the call?" she asked, adding, "We can just plan a stop around that time to give the kids a break, and then we'll be back on the road before we know it."

"I set it up for 11 a.m. thinking we could do just that. We should be in Massachusetts by then."

THE kids were half asleep when we put them in the Tahoe just before 6 a.m. They went right back to sleep, and Brady followed suit. Mary got back into her book but dozed off about a half hour into the drive. For a while, it was just me, a playlist of George Strait tunes, and time to think more deeply about everything that had happened over the last several days. I glanced at the Saint Christopher medal

I had hung from my rearview mirror and then focused on what was out in front of me through the windshield.

An hour later, Mary yawned, stretched, and turned to check on Patrick and Elizabeth. She had packed breakfast sandwiches and handed them out to everyone. I was still sipping from a mug of lukewarm coffee, so the sandwich was a welcome bite.

"Dad, are we going to be able to hike on the Appalachian Trail this weekend?" Patrick asked between bites.

"Pat, we always do," Elizabeth chimed in before I could answer. "Why do you think mom packed our hiking boots and backpacks?"

"That's right, Elizabeth," Mary affirmed. "You're all set up to go."

"Yep," I added, "we should do that on Saturday. Maybe Aunt Annie will come with us."

"How much farther, Dad?" Patrick asked. As I glanced at him in the rearview mirror, I could see him trying to figure out where we were by searching for road signs from the window.

"We're in New York." Then I added in my most encouraging voice, "Still a long way to go, but we will get there."

Patrick caught my eye in the mirror and asked, seemingly out of nowhere, "Dad, how come the mirror is so small, you can hardly see anything in it?"

"Well, Pat," thanks to my conversation with the cabby, I didn't even have to think about how to answer his question, "it's because what is behind isn't as important as what's in front of us. So the windshield is much bigger because what we really need to see is up ahead."

I could see the wheels turning in his mind. Then he asked, "Why isn't what's behind us important?"

"It is Pat," I paused, revisiting my conversation with Ed just the night before. "It's just that if we are always looking behind us, we will miss all the stuff in front of us, the stuff we haven't seen yet, and we wouldn't want to miss anything, would we?"

"I don't want to miss a thing!" Patrick exclaimed enthusiastically.

By the time we saw the "Massachusetts Welcomes You" sign, it was perfect timing. It was almost 11 a.m., and the first rest area was just ahead on the right after entering the state.

The sun was shining on a perfect morning and what was turning out to be a lovely day to travel.

As I pulled off the highway and into a spot open by a set of picnic tables, Mary said, "We'll take Brady for a walk while you take your call."

"Sounds good," I said as I reached behind the seat and grabbed my computer bag. I positioned the computer on the center console, set my notebook on my lap, and collected my thoughts. I logged on to the Zoom call, and everyone joined one by one: Jeff, Pat, Chris, and then Carol.

"The gang's all here," I quipped.

"Jack," Chris asked, "what exactly is the purpose of the call today? Unfortunately, we didn't get much information. Didn't we review what we had going on in detail last week?"

"I know, guys," I tried to answer the question we were all asking as diplomatically as possible. "Bill is concerned that we are going to miss our goal. He should be on any minute, by the way. It looks like we're sitting at 92 percent going into the last quarter . . . and that's just not enough."

"Not enough?" Pat asked rhetorically. "Man, you can't get blood from a rock . . . or something like that."

Before I could respond, Bill's face popped up on the screen.

"Good to see everyone here on time," he said without acknowledging that he was a few minutes late. "Let's get right to it. We are at a crossroads in this company. I've saddled Jack and all of you with a monumental task. We have achieved great growth over the last two years but are not there yet. Even though I recognize our growth has been above industry averages, it's not good enough for the board. So, Jack, break this down for us."

And with that, I went through everything that was going on in each region, just as I had in Friday's meeting last week. Of course, the team already knew that I had asked for detailed reports to be submitted to Kathy tomorrow. Still, I reiterated that for Bill's sake. Then, I launched into the plans for the meeting next week. "Bill has asked that we have an in-person meeting next Thursday. Kathy will make reservations for you for Wednesday night at the Marriott Courtyard a few blocks from the office. I'll have an agenda out to you Monday afternoon. In the meantime, I want you to contact your distributors and remind them of their individual quotas."

I could tell that Jeff looked perturbed. Chris seemed to be jotting notes off to the side, and Pat was inputting information into his phone. "Alright," Carol was the only one to verbally acknowledge the change of plans.

"Plan to arrive by about 4 p.m. next Wednesday, and we'll have a team dinner that evening, nothing fancy." Bill preferred everyone just to have pizza and beer.

"What about flights out?" Pat asked.

"5 p.m. or later," I said. "We'll end our meeting at 3 p.m. sharp to give everyone enough time to get to the airport."

Then Bill circled back to quota, "Team, we are at 92 percent to quota with only 90 days left. I'm sure Jack has communicated to you that anything less than quota is not acceptable. Still, I have to reiterate how important this is for the company and for all of our futures. Every region has to be equally accountable. We need you to work with your distributors to convey a sense of urgency. I don't want to make changes, but we *will* evaluate every region at the end of the year."

The silence on the call was so thick I could cut it with a knife. Of course, everyone would be getting a quarterly review, but I definitely would have taken a different approach to Bill's fear tactic.

"Team, I'm proud of all of you," I did my best to end the meeting positively. "The greatest comeback in the history of sports started with about eight minutes left in the third quarter. I believe in you, and I know we can do it."

"Yeah," Bill jumped in, "and failure isn't an option."

"That's right," again, I tried to steer the tone toward an encouraging one. "Games are won and lost in the last quarter, sometimes in the last few seconds or at the buzzer."

"But we're not going to let this come down to a last-second shot," Bill stipulated. "Jack, have this all prepared in a presentation format for our meeting next week."

"Will do, Bill," I nodded before adding, "Team, I know we're going to pull this out."

With that, everyone left the meeting. I sat there for a minute, staring at the screen. *Why did it feel like Bill had turned the call into a "good cop, bad cop" scenario? At least, I guess I'm the good cop,* I thought to myself.

Mary and the kids had taken turns using the bathroom and walked back toward the Tahoe with Brady as I shut my computer. We couldn't have timed it any better.

"How'd it go?" Mary asked as she opened the passenger door.

"Just great," I said, smiling back at her, "just great."

"Is that a for real 'just great'?" she asked in a playful tone. "Or is it a sarcastic 'just great'?"

"Let's just say it was direct and to the point. Now," I said, eager to change the subject, "let's hit the road and find our little piece of heaven on earth."

A couple hours later, we passed the "Welcome to Maine: The Way Life Should Be" sign.

"It sure is!" we always said when we crossed the bridge from New Hampshire to the "Pine Tree State." Within another few hours, with two sleeping kids in the back, we rolled into Farmington to gas up for the last time at the Irving station. By the time Mary got the groceries and we loaded them in the back, it was nearly 4 p.m. Elizabeth and Patrick awakened at the sound of the back hatch closing and, in unison, asked the question every kid asks on a long road trip: "Are we there yet?"

"We'll be there in about an hour," Mary said with anticipation. I didn't know who was more excited, her or the kids.

"See, Brady," Elizabeth said, "we're almost there, boy."

"Yeah, almost there," Patrick echoed, a notch or two higher on the volume scale as his excitement rose.

I could feel my own excitement rising, as well.

The camp road appeared just over the last set of three small hills. When we pulled off the paved road, it was like we had entered another world, free from the outside influence of our day-to-day grind, almost like we entered another time where things stood still long enough for us to enjoy them, long enough for us to take a deep breath. I looked over at Mary, who had just cracked the window to breathe the fresh air. I could see she felt the same way I did.

It was a beautiful sight as we cornered the east side of the lake, looking back at the sunset over the mountain. Mary commented she could smell the wood stove burning as we pulled into the drive. It was such a delightful surprise to see that Annie was already there and had gotten a fire going.

The words rang in my head like a symphony: *It's the simple things that make a difference.*

# CHAPTER TWELVE

~

# FROM ANNIE'S PERSPECTIVE

I COULD HEAR MY BROTHER, JACK, AND HIS FAMILY coming down the gravel road before I could even see their vehicle. As I stood up from the porch swing, I marveled at how the fall foliage virtually glowed as the sun set on the mountain. By the time I reached the bottom step, the Tahoe had stopped.

"Auntie Annie," Elizabeth yelled as she flung the door open, "it's you!"

"Well, of course, it's me!" I exclaimed. "Do you think I would miss this? I came all this way just to see you and Patrick."

"I knew it, I knew it!"

"And Patrick, look how much you've grown!" It had been quite a while since I had seen my niece and nephew. I was now covered in hugs for what seemed an eternity, loving every minute of it. I waved to Jack and Mary, who looked on with broad smiles. We could all see this visit was long overdue.

The fire had already warmed up the walls of the cabin. I had spaghetti sauce simmering on the gas stove, and the gas lights gave off the familiar soft yellow ambiance that had just the calming effect I was hoping for.

"You sure didn't waste any time, Annie," Jack said as he entered the cabin with bags in each hand. Mary was already unloading the car, and Brady was sniffing everything along the perimeter of the grass all the way down to the lake. Patrick was helping, too, bringing in his bags and carrying them up to the loft area. Elizabeth had her backpack over her right shoulder and her Barbie doll in her hand.

"See, I'm helping too, Mom," she called Mary as she skipped up the stairs.

We settled in for a delicious spaghetti dinner with some garlic bread and Mary's homemade apple pie for dessert. Dinner with family in a special place always seemed to keep us grounded.

Jack and I were always close, practically joined at the hip when we were younger. Though, at times we seemed to get lost in our individual lives, it was such a blessing that we could pick up where we left off. I think he always felt like he needed to watch over me, but unbeknownst to Jack, I think I helped to keep him centered.

He tried to hide the stress of his job, but I knew that when he wasn't talking about it much, the stress level must be high. Mary and I spoke more often than Jack knew and were usually on the same page. Jack couldn't have found a better partner to spend his life with.

With everyone tucked in after 9 p.m., Jack sat in the recliner with one lone gas light behind him, writing in his journal. I was so happy to see him writing again. His journal was always a source of finding clarity. It wasn't long before the soft light and fresh air got the best of him, and he drifted off to sleep. I headed off to bed too.

THE next morning, I awoke at 6:30 a.m., which was late for me. Elizabeth and Patrick were still sound asleep in the loft, and Jack must have woken up in the recliner at some point during the night and gone to bed. However, Mary was already sitting outside on the porch swing with a well-stoked fire in the stove. I poured myself a cup of coffee from the percolator and took a deep breath, filling my lungs with the warm, calming aroma.

"I see you found the coffee," Mary lifted her own mug in salute as I made my way toward the swing.

I sat next to her and we enjoyed a few minutes of comfortable silence, listening to the birds and sipping our coffee.

"Mary," I interrupted our reverie, "I don't want to pry, but how is Jack's job really going?"

"Jack is a great leader and mentor to his team," Mary seemed careful to speak well of Jack. "And he would do anything to help them be successful. He is always about bringing out the best in his team, in everyone for that matter."

"Yes, but, at what price?"

"We have both had to make sacrifices," Mary sighed, "but we do what we have to do. Unfortunately, what is necessary for him means a lot of travel and working late at the office," she admitted. "Oh, he tries hard to fit everything in. Like your mom used to joke with him all the time, he really is a 'Jack of all trades.' I wouldn't say a 'master of none because he does them all well . . . except for the toll that it takes on him physically and emotionally. But he rarely lets anyone in, at least not much, to let you know how he is really doing."

"He has always been like that, thinking he has to carry the weight. I don't see him as often as I used to, but I can see it wearing on him."

We turned to each other almost in unison, getting more comfortable on the swing. "Let me ask you this, Mary," I continued, "you know how much Jack and I loved the farm, right?"

"Yes," Mary replied with some hesitation, "but that was years ago. The farm is like a distant memory. It's been out of the family for years. I can't remember the last time he mentioned it."

"I know, I know," I sighed, "but, Mary, I think it's coming up for sale."

"Really?" Mary exclaimed in surprise, then paused. "What would that have to do with us?"

"Bear with me," I pleaded, intending to make my case, "Jack always used to dream of becoming a horse trainer."

"Well, sure," Mary replied, "he used to talk about it when we were younger, but I think it's just a forgotten dream now."

"If we asked him if there was anything he could do as a job, what do you think he would say?"

"I don't know," Mary hesitated, "but I don't think it would be owning a horse farm. He is too caught up in his sales career now."

"Caught up," I repeated Mary's words. "That's what happens to people. We all get caught up."

"I can tell you this," Mary offered, "he *is* happiest when he returns from the barn with Elizabeth."

"I don't think he has ever stopped dreaming, Mary," I looked at her knowingly. "In fact, I'm willing to bet on it. He's just hiding behind his work. You should at least ask each other what your dreams are."

"Annie, what exactly are you getting at?" Mary asked, searching my face for more answers.

"Let's go for a walk," I stood up.

"Okay," Mary stood to join me. "I feel I may need to clear my head to hear what you have to say."

We walked down the wooded road for the next half hour, sipping our coffee, kicking fallen leaves, and taking in the fresh mountain air. We were more like two close sisters instead of sisters-in-law.

"Here's what I'm thinking, Mary," I said, knowing I couldn't keep talking in generalities. "You work remotely. If Jack were to leave his job . . ."

"Wait, are you kidding me?" Mary retorted.

"Hear me out," I urged. "If you continued to work from home, Jack could start a training business. There isn't a good trainer in that area for miles. Skowhegan would easily draw from Waterville for lessons. We could even make it a breeding facility, which would draw customers from all over the state, maybe even the US."

"I hear what you're saying," Mary weighed her response. "It makes some sense on the surface. But, Annie, that would take a lot of work . . . and a LOT of money!"

"Well, I'm willing to invest in the business side. You and Jack would own the house and the farm."

"Annie, Jack may not even hit his bonus this year, and there isn't all that much equity in the house back in Philly."

As we reached the cross-section in the road, we turned and began to walk back in silence. I could tell Mary was pondering the proposal. I wondered if I had gone too far.

Finally, in a soft voice, Mary said, "Maybe I would have my husband back. We both enjoyed horses, and they were a part of our past, and Elizabeth seems to be following in the same footsteps."

Again, we fell into silence as we walked. It seemed that the more she thought about it, the more the wheels turned in Mary's mind.

Finally, Mary turned to me and said with a hint of cautious optimism, "Annie, I agree. It's worth looking into. I would be on board with it, but It has to be right for Jack . . . for the kids, for you, and for me."

"Of course," I gave her a quick squeeze. "We are a family."

"So . . . when is it going up for sale?" Mary asked.

"I'm not 100 percent sure," I said. "The owners are getting up in years, and a friend who knows them really well said they had been thinking about it for some time and were ready to list it for sale. It could be a month; it could be three months."

"Well," Mary replied as we reached the steps to the cabin, "if you really want to pursue this, then I think it's worth having a conversation with Jack about it."

"I just want you all to be as happy as you can be," I reminded her. "But first, we must find out what's really in his heart."

Jack seemed to be getting up as we entered the cabin with our now empty coffee mugs.

"Good morning, sleepy bones," I elbowed my brother. "Mary, does he always sleep this late?"

"Ha, Ha," Jack gave me his best fake laugh. "Honestly, I think the drive and the conference call yesterday did me in."

"Oh, did you have to stop for a call?" I glanced at Mary.

"We did, we did," Jack sighed as he poured the cream into his coffee, adding, "but it went well, just end of the quarter quota stuff."

Mary and I refilled our mugs and sat at the table on either side of Jack's.

"So, Jack," I asked, launching right in, "how are you liking your position at US Ortho?"

"I like it," he answered quickly without any real thought. "I enjoy the challenge," he added, "but I . . . well, I don't enjoy the stress sometimes."

"Seems like there's been more and more of that lately, doesn't it?" Mary added.

"Maybe," Jack conceded. "But that's the price of leadership. Sometimes I have to make critical decisions that no one else can. These decisions affect my team and even the company. It can feel lonely. But, like I said, that's the price you must pay to be in leadership."

"Oh, I have no doubt you are an amazing leader, Jack," I said encouragingly. "I know your team is lucky to have someone like you. But I think the question is, are you fulfilled while you are in a leadership position? Jack, you can't let your job consume you."

"It doesn't consume me," he said somewhat defensively.

"Maybe 'consume' isn't a good word," I backpedaled just a bit. "But, you're my brother, and I can see how the stress affects you. It's just that I know from experience that when your job becomes a grind, you just do it because you have to . . . and not because you want to," I said, trying not to sound like the bossy, big sister.

"I agree, Annie, but I wouldn't necessarily call my job a 'grind.'" Mary must have caught his eye, "Okay," he added somewhat reluctantly, "maybe a few times I've called it a 'grind.'"

"I guess what I'm getting at is, do you really love it? Do you feel that it's your life's work, what you're meant to do?" I searched Jack's face for an answer.

"Have you ever really asked yourself that question, Jack?" Mary had been quiet to this point.

"Why do I get the feeling you two are up to some of your usual conniving?" Jack's nervous laugh told me he wasn't upset, but he was drawn in to see where the conversation was going.

"We just want you to be truly happy," I assured him.

"Hypothetically speaking," Mary asked cautiously, "if someone asked you what you would do if you could do anything you wanted to, how would you answer?"

"What do you mean?" Jack lifted one brow and looked at us both skeptically.

"What Mary is asking," I clarified, "is what's your dream job?"

"Well . . ." Jack paused. "I haven't thought about that question for a long time. I guess I would want to work with horses."

I saw Mary's jaw drop slightly.

"But I would want to do more than that. I've been reading a book one of the doctors I met while in Texas recommended to me. It's about a fascinating field called 'equine assisted learning.'"

"What is that?" I asked. While his answer didn't surprise me at all, his specificity did.

"It involves working with horses to help businesses build leadership skills in their team members and to bring them closer together."

"Oh, wow!" Mary and I exclaimed in unison.

"I have heard of equine therapy," I continued, "but I haven't heard of programs like that."

"They're gaining popularity, and the business world is just one focus," Jack explained. "But, none of that is going to happen anytime soon . . . or in this lifetime."

"Jack," Mary urged," I think you will want to listen to what Annie has to say."

"Okay," Jack said, slowly pushing his chair back from the table. He stood. "I'm going to need a refill for this one," he held up his empty mug. "I can tell."

"Jack," I said, "I think the old farm is coming up for sale soon."

"What?" I could see that he was caught off guard. "I haven't seen the old farm since Gramps passed."

"I know," I said quietly, as his thoughts trailed back over memories of the farm, as mine had just a couple of weeks before.

"How do you know it's coming for sale?" he finally asked.

"Well," I continued, "a close friend knows the owners who are getting up in years, and the 40 acres are a lot to manage."

"Ladies, listen to me," Jack pleaded with us, "I love that farm and the memories with Gramps, but buying a farm of that size requires money."

"Jack, I know it might seem outlandish at first, but think about it for a minute with some vision," I said as persuasively as I could.

"You could do training like you did when you were younger," Mary jumped in. "I could still work from home and help Annie with teaching lessons part-time."

"Once we got going," I picked back up, "we could contract with other trainers to teach. We could have multiple disciplines, western, English, dressage . . . and even the equine learning you mentioned."

"I think I may need to hire you two as sales representatives," Jack laughed again but less nervously than before. "Look, it's a great business model," Jack shook his head slightly, "but, like I said, there has to be money to back it up. Even then, I would have to leave my job."

"That's true," I agreed. "We all know you are darn good at your job, but I can see that you would excel at running your own business too. But, Jack, we're not asking you if you are good at your work. We're asking you if it is what you really want to be doing for the rest of your life."

"Jack," Mary looked directly at Jack with her piercing blue eyes, "remember what we were discussing the other night?"

"Sure, I do, Mar," he paused. "But are you willing to go that far?"

"Think about it, Jack," Mary said earnestly. "You'd never have to go too far to be home for dinner, throw the ball with Patrick, or ride with Elizabeth. Maybe this is the reset we need."

"You know two against one isn't fair, right?"

"It's called teamwork, Jack," Mary winked at me.

"You know we are your two biggest advocates, right, Jack?"

"I do know that," he smiled wistfully, "and I am grateful for both of you."

"Jack," Mary put her hand on his, "we will be here to support you no matter what you decide to do, no matter what comes of this opportunity."

"And," I added as I gathered up our empty coffee mugs, "we'll be here to give you a swift kick in the derriere when you need it."

Our laughter must have awoken Patrick and Elizabeth.

"What's for breakfast, Daddy?" Elizabeth called sleepily while walking down the stairs.

"How about French toast?" Jack called back.

"Yay, my favorite!" she exclaimed as she jumped off the last step. "Just don't make them too eggy," she added as she approached the table.

"I won't," he kissed her on the top of her head. "I'll be sure to make them just right for you."

"Dad is there enough for me to have four with a lot of syrup," Patrick asked, not too far behind his sister.

"Patrick," Jack tousled his son's hair, "if you can eat four, you got it."

I couldn't help but think that it seemed like the load on Jack's shoulders may have already lightened a bit.

"Ladies," Jack concluded before he headed into the kitchen for chef duty, "if the farm is going to come up for sale, and if both of you are in, I'm willing to consider it. But right now, I have a sales team to manage. I have to get through this last quarter. So, if you two have time to do the research, we can pull numbers together to see if it would even be feasible."

"Jack, do you remember what Mom used to say?" I hadn't wanted to use our mother's words to pressure him, but now that he had agreed to at least consider the options, I tried to encourage him about the possibilities. "She would say, 'Listen to your heart, and your dreams will follow.'"

"She did say that, didn't she?" he nodded. "You know, Annie, it's so good to be together again. We shouldn't wait so long next time. Besides, I appreciate the advice of my older and *wiser* sister."

"I'm going to ignore the part about me being older," I gave him my best glare, "but I'm glad I could offer a little different perspective."

# CHAPTER THIRTEEN

~

# THE FARM

L ISTEN TO YOUR HEART, AND YOUR DREAMS WILL *follow.* Annie had reminded me of the words that mom used to say so often, and those words kept rolling around in my mind. *Stay true to who you are.* My mother's words aligned with the message I heard over and over on my trip to Dallas.

Everyone else was still asleep, but I had percolated some coffee and was standing on the dock with a steaming mug and Brady by my side. The lake mirrored the mountain's reflection so perfectly that the images were indistinguishable, one and the same.

I couldn't believe that Sunday was already upon us. We had spent a glorious weekend taking great walks along the gravel camp roads that were never heavily traveled. We also did the hike along the Appalachian Trail the kids were looking forward to. A few cold nights had done their work, and the leaves covering the mountainside created a mesmerizing canvas of brilliant reds and yellows. Then, of course, we raked up the leaves that had already fallen around the cabin so the kids, and Brady, could jump in them. Brady had been in heaven, following Patrick and Elizabeth everywhere, only stopping occasionally to take a snooze on my lap. We spent Saturday afternoon carving pumpkins on the picnic table and lit them up just as the sun was fading away. We enjoyed red hot dogs, a staple in Maine, and followed them up with hot chocolate to ward off the chill.

*It's the simple things that make a difference.* It really is, I thought to myself, but, more than that, it's family that allows those simple things to make all the difference. I couldn't help but wonder if maybe Annie and Mary were on to something. One question led to another, and I asked if I could continue the race to the top. *Am I really being true to myself?* I wasn't ready to make that decision yet, not willing to jump off the cliff into a lake of unknown depth, but the hook might just be set.

After we had closed the cabin, Elizabeth and Patrick showered Annie with enough hugs to last a lifetime . . . or at least until the next time we saw her.

"Jack," Annie said as she was about to get into her Jeep, "I'll start looking into the financial feasibility of buying the farm when I get back. After that, who knows what could happen."

"Ok," I said, "I'll leave the ball in your court."

"I love you, Jack."

"I love you, too, Annie."

With our goodbyes said, we drove our vehicles to the main road and waved before heading our separate ways.

"Jack," Mary began, "thank you so much. This trip was exactly what we needed. The kids had such a wonderful time, and so did I."

"I did too, I did too," I replied. "What was your favorite part of the trip?" I asked the kids as I looked back at them in the rearview mirror.

Elizabeth exclaimed, "The leaves, Dad, jumping in the leaves!"

Patrick thought for a minute and then added, "Everything, just everything . . . except I wish we could have stayed longer."

"Me too, Pat, me too," I replied. "Someday, we'll spend more than just a few days."

"Promise?"

"I promise, Pat, I promise. Wait and see."

"Yay! I want to spend a whole week next summer so we can go fishing."

"Ok," I said, "it's a deal."

"Jack, you better start planning as soon as we get home because that little man has a memory like a steel trap, and he will not let you forget."

"Well, Mary, I figure if I make that commitment now, it is more likely to happen. This weekend is a perfect example of how the simple things have made a difference."

"Jack," Mary's voice sounded almost musical, "there may be hope for you yet."

There was little doubt that we were both more relaxed than we had been on the way up to the cabin. *How could we not be?* I thought to myself, reliving the warmth from the wood stove, the smell of the leaves, and the feel of the fresh mountain air.

"Do me a favor, Jack?" Mary broke into my thoughts.

"If I say, 'Anything for you,' will I get myself in trouble?" I glanced at her. "I mean, seeing how you and Annie ganged up on me."

"No, Jack," she punched me playfully, "but the backroad is coming up in a couple of miles. If we are even considering the farm, don't you think we ought to ensure it's still in good shape, at least from the outside? So, that's the favor I'm asking: Drive by and see what it looks like."

I put up a brief counter-argument, knowing she would win, so I took the left turn when the road sign came up. We drove on in silence for a few minutes. It was as if the car knew where we were going and was on autopilot.

"Jack, you're awfully quiet," Mary interrupted my thoughts.

"I'm just going through a bit of nostalgia seeing all the old farms I remember as a kid. It's been years since I've been on this road."

As we came to a small hill about four miles down the road, the pavement turned to dirt, just as I remembered it. Then, like something from a storybook or a childhood dream, there it was, the old, white Cape Cod farmhouse. Coming up the hill toward the mailbox, I could see a man walking out to get the mail.

"That must be the owner," Mary said. "Do you think we should stop?"

"It must be," I said as we approached the driveway. Then, in a fleeting memory, I remembered we never called it the driveway; it was always the "door yard." I don't know why we called it that, but that's what I remembered.

As we slowed down, Mary rolled down the window.

"Are you lost?" the gentleman asked in a distinctive Maine accent.

He was an older man with a rather rugged complexion from all his days in the sun. He sported coveralls and a Carhartt jacket well suited for work on the farm. He stood about six feet tall, and you could tell from his build that he was no stranger to hard work. Farm work could be demanding and would keep you in shape for sure.

"No," I projected my voice through Mary's window. "We were just driving by admiring the place. My grandparents used to own it a long, long time ago."

"Are you a Kaneen?" he asked, his eyes sparkling with interest.

"Yes, I'm Jack, Jack Kaneen."

"You're young, Jack? I heard about you. I'm Bob Marshall. I bought this place from your grandmother after your grandfather passed years ago. You're welcome to look around if you have a few minutes?"

"Sure," Mary said before I could even get a word out. "That's very kind of you."

"Turn into the door yard, and I'll see where my wife is." As

I hesitantly pulled in, Bob turned toward the barn, calling out, "Noreen? We have company. You'll never guess in a million years who it is."

As I shut down the Tahoe, Patrick, Elizabeth, and Brady got out, their eyes wide in anticipation of our side trip.

"Dad, do they have horses here?" Elizabeth asked.

"It's a farm, Elizabeth," Patrick answered. "I bet they have horses . . . and cows too."

"Yes, son, we have both," Bob laughed good-naturedly.

"See, I told you!" Patrick exclaimed proudly.

"Mom, can we see them?" Elizabeth begged.

"We just got here," Mary whispered, "but maybe before we leave."

Just then, Noreen emerged from the barn.

"Hello," she said in a soft voice. Then, before anyone could reply, she continued, "Why you are the image of your grandfather!"

"So, you know who this is?" Bob asked with surprise.

"Bob, have you ever seen anyone who looked as much like old Jack Kaneen as this young man?"

"Well, I would say he looks like a young Jack Kaneen," Bob laughed, patting me on the back.

"Why don't you come in for a cup of tea?" Noreen suggested.

"Oh, that would be lovely," Mary responded again before I could say a word.

Stepping inside, I could hardly believe how the place looked much the same as I remembered. We sat down in the kitchen while Noreen put on the tea.

"Mr. Marshall, it's nice to see you have kept the farm in such good condition," I said as I continued to look around at the walls and old wooden cupboards just as I remembered them.

"Please, call us Bob and Noreen. Jack, your grandparents kept this place up for over 50 years. We had something extraordinary to live up to."

"Well, thank you for that. I hope we're not imposing," I said. "We were just planning to drive by."

"You folks have come a long way to be just driving by," Noreen said as she began to pour the hot tea from the kettle.

"Well, if we are being honest," Mary said, "Jack's sister, Annie, who still lives in the area, thought you might be getting ready to sell, so I asked Jack to take a little detour on the way home from our cabin up here."

"Well, if *we* are being honest," Bob winked at Noreen, "we know your sister's friend, Muriel, and she thought you might have an interest after talking with her, so she passed the information on to us. In fact, I was kind of hoping it was you when I saw your SUV coming over the hill."

"Really?" Mary and I exclaimed in unison.

"Well, I hope you don't think we're trying to pry you for information," I said. "We really were just planning to drive by for a look."

"Not at all," Noreen smiled. "It's so nice to actually meet you."

"Jack," Bob added, "just the fact that you and your family are sitting here in this kitchen tells me something. Noreen and I have talked about how nice it would be if the farm ended up back in the Kaneen family."

"Well, Bob," I said, setting my cup of tea on its saucer with a clink, "Annie just told us over the weekend about the possibility of the farm coming up for sale. But, of course, a lot would have to happen for us to even consider it."

"I understand," Bob replied. "I know the farm will go to whoever it is supposed to. But you know what they say: Sometimes things are just meant to be."

"You said you have some horses?" Mary asked, with some prodding from Elizabeth.

"We have two," Noreen smiled.

"And a few chickens and an ornery rooster named Ajax that's around here somewhere," Bob added. "The old bird gets a presidential pardon every Thanksgiving." We all laughed. Bob had a great sense of humor.

"Tell you what, kids," Noreen said as she motioned to Mary, "why don't we go down to the pasture and see the horses? Maybe even Ajax will come out to say hi."

"Yay!" Patrick jumped up. "Come on, Elizabeth! This is so cool!"

With that, the screen door off the kitchen slammed behind Mary, Noreen, and the kids.

After a moment of quiet, Bob said, "Jack, this farm became our lives nearly 20 years ago. I was a young man like you when we decided to buy it. I wasn't sure I could do it, but I took the chance."

"What made you take the chance?"

"I had some good counsel," he smiled. "I used to be an ironworker. An older gentleman I worked with said, 'Bob, if it's your dream to own that farm, then you need to stay true to yourself. If you don't, you will regret it when it's time for God to call you home.'"

"Wow!" I shook my head, "That reminds me of someone I know who would probably say something similar, but that's another story."

"Jack, you don't want to leave anything on the table in this life. I don't know you personally, but I think I'm a good judge of character. Be true to yourself. Search out who you really are and what you are truly meant to do. Don't settle for anything less than that."

As we got up to walk outside, I shook Bob's hand. "I can't

thank you enough for your candidness and wisdom," I said. "Now, let's rally the troops or wrangle the herd. We have a long drive to get back to Philly."

CHAPTER FOURTEEN

~

# THE HOME STRETCH

H AVING ENJOYED SOME GREAT FOOD AND FUN conversation with the team at Pat's Pizza and Pasta off of Broad Street, I sent them all back to the Courtyard for a restful evening. I called Mary when I got back in the car to let her know that I planned to stop by the office to review the presentations and agenda one last time before the meeting the next day.

Knowing I had done all I could, I shut my computer down and sat at my desk in the familiar silence of the office at night after everyone had gone home. Despite any doubts I might have had earlier in the quarter, I felt confident that I had the right people on our bus and that we were going in the right direction. Each person really had given it their best. Leading a team and doing everything I could to bring out their best and to make them better was fulfilling . . . *But is it enough?* I had to ask myself.

Following our visit to the cabin, I felt reinvigorated. Having read *The Seven Habits of Highly Effective People* more than a couple of times, I could see that my time at the cabin had been just like Stephen Covey's analogy of "sharpening the saw."

Mary and Annie made some valid points over the weekend, and I couldn't help but ask myself if I had been so caught up in my work that I forgot what I really wanted. Had I allowed my race to the top to consume me so much that I had been missing what would really make me happy?

I had hoped I might hear that familiar whistle tonight so I could talk to Ed about all that was running through my mind. In fact, part of me wondered if that was the real reason I had come back to the office after dinner. But the floor was quiet. Slightly disappointed, I grabbed my coat and briefcase and headed toward the elevator.

When the doors opened, there stood Ed.

"Going down?" he asked.

"Not if you're coming up," I remarked. "I thought I had missed you tonight."

"You know, I was hoping I might run into you too," Ed said as he rolled his cart off the elevator. "You haven't worked late the last few nights."

"Well, someone told me the simple things make the difference."

"And you took that to heart, did you?" Ed asked, feigning surprise.

"I'm trying to," I nodded sincerely.

"I need to get to work, Jack, but I would love to hear about your trip up to God's country if you don't mind talking while I mop?"

"Not at all."

"I usually start right here so that I can mop myself out the elevator door each night," he chuckled as he lifted his mop out of the soapy water.

"Ed, I'm so glad I went to Maine," I launched into everything I wanted to tell him. "It was a long drive, but it was just what we needed."

"I'm glad for you, Jack, I really am," his voice sounded a little reminiscent. "Didn't the sign used to say 'Welcome to Maine: The Way Life Should Be?'"

"Still does," I replied.

"Nothing like going to a place as beautiful as that where life is simple, the air is fresh, and the mountains . . . well, the mountains tell us a lot without ever saying a word."

"They sure do," I nodded. "I tell you, the weather was great, cool nights, the wood stove, long walks . . ."

"Sounds wonderful."

". . . and an ambush by my wife and sister."

"An ambush?" he asked with a laugh. "Now, how does a Marine walk into an ambush?"

"Ha-ha," I replied in jest. "They have had a lot of experience in 'tactical warfare.'"

"So, tell me about this ambush."

"Where do I begin? My sister Annie found out that the old family farm might be coming up for sale. Well, they talked about it, as women will do, and it seems they are worried about me and the stress I have been under the last few years. They asked me to think about whether it's what I really want to be doing?"

"Oh, my! They did plan an ambush, didn't they?"

"I'll say," I grinned.

"So, how did you answer their question?"

"Which one?" I laughed.

"What is it that you really want?"

"Well, that's a loaded question," I shook my head. "It could cover a lot of different areas."

"It could, you're right," Ed conceded. "It's like we were talking about last week: What does it mean to be true to yourself? Have you given that any more thought, Jack?"

"Actually, I have, Ed. I've given it a lot of thought," I took a deep breath. "I think it means not losing sight of who I am. It goes back to our Marine code, Ed: 'Semper Fidelis.' Always Faithful— faithful to God, family, country, and especially where I came from. But it also depends on where I'm going and who I take with me on the journey. It's staying true to my values and being present enough to know what's important to my family and those who care about me

. . . and what's important to me."

"Now there's something, Jack," he stopped mopping for a moment and looked straight at me. "What's important to you?"

"Well, family is the most important, although I realize I haven't been making them my top priority. And success is a lot less important than I've been living like it is."

"Let me ask you this, Jack if you could do anything and make a living doing it, what would it be?"

"Are you sure you aren't conspiring with Mary and Annie? They asked me the very same question at the cabin."

"So, what was your answer?"

"I said I'd work with horses. My grandfather introduced me to them when I was just a boy. It was his life's work, his calling. You could tell. It wasn't long before I lived and breathed the same dream."

"It sounds like that's pretty clear in your mind, Jack."

"Like it was yesterday," I forced myself back to the present. "But you grow up, and those times become a distant memory. This is what I do now. I'm a VP of Sales and good at it."

"I have no doubt that you are good at it, Jack. I'm good at mopping floors, but it's not my life's work."

"What *do* you consider your life's work?"

"Well, I've gone about it many different ways," Ed stopped mopping again, "but my life's work, what keeps me going, is helping people."

"How did you find what you were meant to do?"

"My career advice is simple, son," he looked right into my eyes. "Listen to your heart, and your dreams will follow."

"That's exactly what Annie said this weekend. It's like another of those mantras I repeatedly hear everywhere I turn."

"Jack, why should it surprise you that people who care about you see a similar picture? They see the real you even when the clouds of distraction in your mind won't let you see yourself."

By this time, Ed and I had worked our way down the cubicles on the far side of the elevator and were turning the corner by Bill's office.

"So, tell me, Jack," his question broke into the comfortable silence, "if you had that farm back in your family, what would you do with it?"

"Well, I would start training young horses and selling them to people who wanted to show them or ride them for pleasure. Annie and Mary said that they would help start a lesson program. Eventually, we would breed and train high-quality Quarter Horses. But I would also want to start this unique type of training called equine-assisted learning. I've done a fair amount of research on it since Dr. Johnson shared an article with me while I was in Texas. I would have businesses and teams come in, and we would do team building and leadership development. It would be totally out of the classroom."

"I have never heard of that training before, Jack, but it sounds exciting."

"It would take a lot of work, but I think it is something I would be really good at. It is a career that could combine my love for horses with my business skills."

"I can tell your wheels are turning. Sounds like you need to get back in the saddle again."

"Oh, I almost forgot, our trainer wants me to try a new mare she's bringing in. Mary's all for it, and, of course, Elizabeth would love for us to be able to ride together."

"That's great, Jack!" Ed's face beamed as if he genuinely shared my excitement. "As I said, I agree with your mother's words: 'Listen to your heart, and your dreams will follow.'"

"Ed," I looked at him inquisitively, "I never said that it was my mother who used to say that to Annie and me."

"Jack," he chuckled, "we both know that most words of wisdom come from our parents."

"Annie is a lot like our mom, that's for sure," I let his answer go as just another coincidence that seemed to happen in every conversation I had with Ed.

"Keep listening to her, Jack," he said as he dunked his mop back into the water. "Just like Mary, she cares about you. And keep asking yourself these questions. The right answers will come, and everything else will fall into place when they do."

I thought about the farm on the drive home. I allowed myself to dream a little—a vision for training, working with the horses and creating a program that could help any team or business leader be the best version of themselves. I could imagine helping not just one team but several teams and leaders each year, a way to make even more of a difference. It encompassed what was important to me and what I was good at family, horses, and business. Could that be the answer I was looking for? *Could that really be my life's work?*

AS I stood at the conference room door, it was hard to believe it had been a whole week since the Zoom call I'd taken on the road. It seemed like the blink of an eye. Then, the elevator bell rang, and Pat made his way toward me with his computer bag.

"Morning, Pat," I shook his hand. "I know I said this last night, but you look great!"

"Thanks, Jack," he smiled. "It's good to be back to full force.

Although, I tell you, getting in a run on the treadmill this morning was an extra effort on eastern time."

As the bell rang again, Pat was pulling his computer out of his bag. Carol, Chris, and Jeff emerged from the elevator laughing, and I could tell that our team dinner had helped with their feeling of camaraderie.

"Morning, Jack," Chris called.

"Hope you all got some rest last night," I said as they each found their seat, and they all responded in the affirmative.

"I want to thank you all again for coming in today," I wanted them to know that I appreciated the extra effort. "It was great to get to spend some time together in person last night and catch up apart from work."

Just then, Bill strode through the door, taking his usual seat at the head of the table. "Alright, team, give it to me straight," he said simply. I could feel the atmosphere in the room shift from casual and friendly to slightly on edge.

Once I had finished the opening I'd prepared, Carol, who was scheduled to present first, seemed anxious to get her report underway.

As her first slide popped up on the screen, we all read in large print, "GOOD NEWS!"

"Okay," Pat said, urging her on.

"What's this good news?" Jeff voiced the anticipation for all of us.

Without saying a word, she flipped to the next slide: "Maine Medical Center is Back."

We erupted with cheers.

"I didn't see that coming, but we'll take it!" I exclaimed.

Bill's voice bellowed louder than the rest, "Now that's the kind of news we want to hear! Great job, Carol!"

We filled the room with well-deserved applause. Needless to say, I was shocked but grateful.

Carol finished her presentation covering other business and her fourth-quarter plan.

"Carol," I said as she took her seat, "this couldn't be better news. You have worked incredibly hard, and you kept going back when they turned you away at the door."

"Agreed," Bill echoed. "Great job staying on top of this."

"Well, we might just as well keep adding to the good news," Chris stood up next for his presentation and loaded his first slide. "I got word that we made the value analysis meeting this month."

Again, we cheered.

"It's next week, and, with the support we have, we will likely be approved. I have submitted all the documents they need. If we are approved, the surgeons will be doing cases before the end of the month, which is much sooner than I ever anticipated. We just need to ensure we get the sets ready, and I've already given the list to operations."

"That's awesome news, Chris! You have been working hard to get this in."

"Well, it's not done yet, but we are first and goal, for sure!" Chris added with confidence.

Right about when Chris finished his presentation, Chad poked his head in the door.

"Chad," I said as I waved him in, "Chris here was just talking about sending a list to operations for those instruments." Then, I turned my attention toward the team, "You all know Chad Hanson. He was in a design meeting earlier this morning, but I asked him to stop by to update us on the long-awaited kinematic alignment instruments that Dr. Waverly has been designing. So, Chad, I'm going to turn it over to you. We've all been looking forward to your update."

"Well, here they are!"

This time I knew the silence in the room was interest and excitement rather than concern over Bill's reaction.

With each successive slide, Chad brought an instrument out of his bag, reviewing each one individually and passing them around for us to see up close as he talked about usage and specifications. I watched in delight as the team members looked like children on Christmas morning with new toys Santa had just created at his workshop. Even Bill seemed impressed.

"I know Dr. Waverly will be extremely pleased with these, Chad. He has been anxiously awaiting their arrival as if they were his babies. I'll call him over lunch and set up a time for us to take them to him early next week. Of course, he will want to begin planning his patient seminars and scheduling surgeries once he has the instruments in hand."

"Us?" Chad looked puzzled.

"Sure," I said as I stood up to shake Chad's hand. "You should be the one to present them to him in person." I glanced at Bill, wondering but not really caring if he thought this was another example of my hand-holding.

"That'd be great!" Chad seemed genuinely pleased.

"Thanks again, Chad, for all your hard work on this project. Okay, team," I said enthusiastically, turning my attention toward the table, "this is really exciting news! Let's all review the list of where we can go to get these tools in the hands of surgeons and get them deployed as soon as possible. By Monday after next, I need a list from each of you of cases scheduled with these sets through the end of the year."

"Let's make that a week from today," Bill didn't say it as a suggestion.

"I can give you a PowerPoint and some sample instruments

when needed," Chad followed up.

"Chad, why don't you just share that PowerPoint with the team," I recommended, "and they can contact you directly to get the sample instruments."

"Will do," Chad agreed as he gathered up his instruments.

"Why don't you stay for lunch, Chad," I said. "We've had a very productive morning, and we're just about to take a break. The food should be here any minute, and there will be plenty." I knew that Bill never stayed for our catered lunches, but we always ordered enough just in case.

"That'd be great," Chad moved toward the vacant seat at the far end of the table. "I can answer any team questions about the new instruments."

"Alright, team," Bill interjected right on cue. "I'm going to leave you to it. I may or may not be back for the afternoon briefings. I want you to know that your numbers this month are showing promise." Then he added, "I'll expect a double down this last quarter, okay?"

Everyone nodded.

After lunch, we heard from Jeff and Pat, whose presentations both went well. Jeff was confident he would continue to "hold serve," which was his favorite term, but appropriate considering his success and staying close to his distributors to ensure nothing fell through the cracks. Pat was still riding high over our commitment from Dr. Johnson.

Bill managed to stick his head back just as everyone gathered their computers and bags. Then, dressed for what looked like a tennis match at his club, he shared his parting words. "Just remember that the board is looking for 98 percent to quota for those bonuses . . . but you know they aren't really happy unless it's 100 percent. So let's get those numbers!"

"Sure thing." "Will do." "You bet." "Of course." Everyone gave their assent.

Wanting to keep everyone on time for their Uber to the airport, I kept my concluding words to a minimum and kept numbers out of it. "Thank you all again for your continued commitment to our goals and your 'never say never attitude. We're in the home stretch, and you are really showing your grit. We didn't come this far to quit."

Kathy gathered her folders, the last beside me, out of the conference room. "What a difference a week makes!" she said enthusiastically. "I guess it shows you don't bet against Jack Kaneen!"

"It's not me, Kathy," I replied. "It's the team, all of you. I'm seeing the best you all have to give now, and, as a leader, I couldn't be prouder."

"You're a modest man, Jack," Kathy said.

"Not modest, just honest," I said. And with that, I headed to my office to phone Mary.

"Hi, Jack," she answered, "how did the big meeting go?"

"An amazing thing happened, Mary," I couldn't contain the excitement in my voice. "We finished stronger than I had anticipated for the month. I won't say some of the crew was sandbagging or that Bill's Zoom call on Thursday had made a huge difference, but, regardless, we gained a point toward quota. And, on top of that, the surgery schedule is already strong going into the new month."

"Jack, that's wonderful!" Mary exclaimed. "I'm so proud of you!"

"I just need to stay a while to ensure I have a good handle on the day and send a follow-up response while it's still fresh in my mind. I shouldn't be much longer."

"I understand," Mary replied. Her patience always amazed me. Of course, maybe it helped that I had actually made it home for dinner Monday and Tuesday nights. "And if you don't make it home by the time we eat, I'll keep your plate warm. The kids and I have been enjoying having you home for dinner again more often."

"I have too, Mary. I'll let you know when I'm on my way . . ."

"Oh, by the way, Jack," Mary said suddenly remembering, "Alissa called and said that the new horse has arrived, and she wants to make sure you will be out on Saturday with Elizabeth."

"That's great, Mar! Maybe we should all go Saturday. What do you think?"

"I think that sounds perfect," Mary replied. "It will be a welcomed weekend."

As I hung up the phone, I was reminded of how blessed I was.

# CHAPTER FIFTEEN

~

# DREAMER

C'MON, SAGE," ELIZBETH CALLED AS SHE approached the paddock. Sage whinnied like clockwork, and the two met by the gate. It was so much fun to watch their relationship grow.

Elizabeth brought Sage in through the large side door, and Mary, Patrick, and I followed a little ways behind.

"Hi, Mr. Kaneen," Alissa called cheerfully. "Do you want to look at her before we start Elizabeth's lesson?"

I felt a bit like a kid in a candy store approaching the stall. But, with just one glance, I could already tell that she was a beautiful Quarter Horse, black with a white snip on her face and four perfect white socks. She was tall, just over 16 hands, and had kind but confident eyes.

"Let me get her out," Alissa said, reaching for the halter.

"Okay," I replied, already mesmerized by her beauty. "I'll brush her and get to know her a bit."

"Is that our new horse?" Patrick asked.

"Not so fast," I reminded him. "We're just looking at her."

"Well, Mom said she was perfect for you."

*Out of the mouth of babes!* "Mom told you that, did she?" I looked at Mary somewhat quizzically.

"Yep, when we came to look at her yesterday," Patrick continued without the slightest hesitation.

Alissa's eyes widened as she put her hand to her mouth to stifle a giggle.

"Well," Mary grinned, "I guess Patrick let the cat . . . or the *horse* . . . out of the bag."

"Alissa says her name is Dreamer, just like in the Disney movie about the racehorse," Patrick kept going.

"Well, I think that name suits her fine. What do you think, Mary?" I couldn't help ribbing her a little now that I knew about their little recon trip.

"I think they ganged up on you for this one, Mr. Kaneen," Alissa smiled. But seeing Dreamer in front of me, I was entirely on board with the planning that had obviously gone on behind the scenes.

While Mary helped Elizabeth get Sage tacked up, I spent some time brushing Dreamer.

I could see Pat watching cautiously, not knowing what to make of the horse.

"Pat, would you like to brush her?" I asked.

"Umm," Pat contemplated, "would it be okay, Dad?"

"Sure, it will," I encouraged, holding the brush to him. "Come on over."

"See, Pat, she really likes you," I assured him as he lightly stroked Dreamer's neck. "Would you like to ride her after I'm done?"

"Really?" he asked, his eyes lighting up.

"Of course," I promised as we continued to brush Dreamer together.

Elizabeth's lesson went well, and she seemed to be making progress each week.

Once Sage was put back out, Elizabeth and Alissa returned to where we were.

"I like her, Dad," Elizabeth said as if she had been part of the whole conspiracy . . . which she had. "Mom does too."

"She does, does she?" I asked playfully. "Well, you'll just have to tell Mom I agree." Her smile widened. "Alissa, do you mind if I spend some time in the round pen to get to know her before I get on?" I asked.

"No, not at all," Alissa replied. "I'll get you a lunge line."

"I won't need it," I said. "I'm just going to let her go at liberty and see what happens."

"What does 'at liberty' mean, Dad?" Elizabeth asked.

"A horse at liberty can travel free," I explained, "no halter, no lunge line, no tack."

Letting a horse travel around in a circle in the round pen at liberty without a lunge line was something I hadn't seen anyone do since Elizabeth began taking lessons. I guessed it might look a bit out of the ordinary as I let Dreamer move unrestricted in a controlled environment. I even surprised myself by asking Alissa if I could do it. It was ingrained somewhere in my memory, and I could tell it was all coming back to me moment by moment.

Dreamer was a willing participant and walked over to the round pen, following by my side.

She immediately trotted off to the other side of the ring once I removed her halter. She stood proud and majestic, watching me from the other side as I picked up the lunge whip by the gate and stepped into the center of the ring. I would only use the whip as an extension of my arm as a directional tool.

It was like meeting a person for the first time. She was watching me; I was watching her. She was whinnying and snorting at me; I was encouraging her, telling her what a good girl she was.

I began by talking to her, being present in the moment, and watching her actions. Which way her ears were turned would tell me whether she was paying attention. If they were turned back and against her head and her back was round and hollow, it would mean she was angry or at least not comfortable with the situation. I knew that, eventually, if she began to trust me, she would drop her head, turn her ears toward me, and relax her tail rather than swishing back and forth. Another sure sign that she was getting comfortable would be licking her lips.

I asked her to cantor from the trot and then back to the trot, one way and then the other way. It seemed I was using words I hadn't used in years, reliving what I had all but forgotten. Everything else seemed to fade away, and it was as if I was cast into another world. There were no phone calls, interruptions, or stress, just Dreamer and me in the present. As she traveled around me, I got flashes of Chance, my first gelding, and me doing the same exercises long ago.

I lost track of time, and while it seemed like a half hour, it was only about 15 minutes. But, in this short period, something happened. When I asked her to walk, Dreamer gave me all the signs that a relationship was forming. She began to lick her lips and hang her head low. I knew then she was starting to trust me. Trust is vital in any relationship, and with a horse, it can make all the difference.

*What was it Dr. Johnson had said at our dinner meeting?* "Horses live in the moment and help us do the same."

I asked Dreamer to walk again, and then with a verbal "Woah," she stopped and turned toward me. I dropped the lunge whip and turned my body away from her but not totally turning my back on her. It was up to her now. Did she want to solidify the relationship? All through a few minutes in the round pen, we had established boundaries. Now, I was silently asking her to trust me. She stood there licking her lips and blowing out of her nostrils a big sigh. Then, without hesitation, she walked over to me and rested her head on my right shoulder. I knew at that moment we would make a great team. She was taking long, slow breaths showing me how relaxed she was, and I timed my breaths to coincide with her as she nuzzled close to me. It was just the two of us.

After a minute or two, I thought I would test the relationship. If she followed me around the pen, we would be totally connected. I kept saying, "That's a good girl. That's a good girl." Then, I asked her quietly if she would like to take a little walk, and, with that, I stepped outward with my left leg away from her so that I wouldn't walk into her space and violate the trust we had just established. It was like she was glued to my side, walking to the left and then zigzagging slightly as we walked together. I was reliving a piece of my past I had never really forgotten. I had just misplaced it, but now, I had found it again in this space and time.

Suddenly, like being awakened from a dream, I heard clapping. When I looked up, I could see that Dreamer, and I had attracted quite the audience. At the gate were Mary, Elizabeth, Patrick, Alissa, and Donna Carlisle, the stable owner who had joined the small audience. Donna had grown up riding and showing Quarter Horses, and Pennsylvania Equestrian Center had always been her dream.

"What's all the commotion, Alissa?" I heard Donna ask.

"Mr. Kaneen has some skills we didn't know about," Alissa responded.

"Well, it seems like he knows what he's doing there in the round pen," Donna observed.

"He never once mentioned it to any of us," Alissa replied.

"Looking good, Mr. Kaneen," Donna called. "You really know what you're doing out there!"

"Mr. Kaneen," Alissa sounded amazed, "I had no idea you could do that!"

"Me either, Jack," Mary's voice reflected awe. "I knew you had worked with horses, but . . . I had no idea. That was amazing!"

"When were you going to let us all in on your hidden talents?" Donna asked.

Dreamer and I just stood there for a moment. "It helps when you have a horse as good as this one. She really does have a special quality," I said as I pushed the dirt back and forth with my boot, feeling a little shy from the unexpected attention. "I guess the true test will be how she is under saddle. Huh, girl?" I said, brushing her neck with my hand.

"After that surprise, Mr. Kaneen," Alissa said enthusiastically, "I can't wait to see how you two look going around the ring."

"I can't either," Mary added with a smile.

Climbing in the saddle was surreal after so many years. I immediately thought, *How did I get away from this?* Once I got comfortable, Alissa had me trot her around and then cantor. Living up to her name, Dreamer was a *dream* to ride. She floated along gracefully at the cantor. When I asked her to change her lead from right to left for the first time, she almost anticipated it, so I barely had to ask. Let's just say she made a middle-aged, out-of-shape man look pretty good.

"I think she likes you," Elizabeth called out from the observation area at the end of the arena. Alissa agreed, watching our every move from the middle of the ring.

"She looks excellent, and you have her framed up very nicely at the trot. I like how her head tucks in, and she is really driving the trot from the hind end, which is exactly what we want to see. But what do you think, Mr. Kaneen? That's what really matters."

"I think she is wonderful. But, even more than that, she has a kind eye and a great disposition. She doesn't really care about anything else going on around her."

"She is a great fit," Alissa concluded. "I think you could do a lot with her, Mr. Keenan, and she is only six years old, just getting started."

"I agree, Alissa," I replied. "And it looks like I'm going to be coming here a lot more often, so, please, call me Jack. Everyone else does. Can we plan to set up a lesson on Saturdays following Elizabeth's?"

"I think that will work, Mr., ah . . . Jack," Alissa responded over another round of applause from Mary and the kids. "I'll put it on the schedule."

"Alright, Pat, would you like a turn now?" I called out to Patrick. Again, his eyes lit up as Alissa walked him to where I had dismounted.

I lifted Pat under his arms and into the saddle. His eyes were wide as could be, and, for a second, he didn't know what to make of it all.

"Here, hold on to the saddle," Alissa guided his hands, "and don't worry about the stirrups."

"Would you like to take a little walk?" I asked him.

"Okay," was all he could say, the excitement evident in his voice.

Pat, Dreamer, and I walked around the ring together in a moment that any dad would relish.

"Pat, horses are amazing animals," I told him. "If you treat them well, they will treat you well too. Of course, there is a lot to it, but I bet you would be a great rider."

"You think so, Dad?" he asked somewhat nervously. "You think I could do it just like Elizabeth?"

"Think?" I repeated. "I know you could," I said, my voice instilling confidence in him.

"Yay, Patrick!" Elizabeth cheered as we returned to the end of the ring. "You did it!"

"Good job!" Alissa called.

"You look great, Patrick," Mary said, "a real natural."

His eyes beamed at all of the encouragement.

It was a great way to end the day at the barn. I never even thought Patrick would have an interest like Elizabeth did. It always seemed like Patrick was only interested in sports, but then, I had never really approached it with him, I thought to myself as we untacked Dreamer and brushed her. Patrick and Elizabeth each gave her some apple oat treats, and we tucked her away comfortably in her new stall.

"I didn't stand a chance, did I?" I asked Mary as we walked back to the Tahoe to head home.

"I know this is going to be so good for you!" Mary replied. "It's what you have wanted even though you didn't realize it," she winked.

"Mary, you are always looking out for me," I grabbed her hand.

"I'm looking out for *us*, Jack, just like you are," Mary replied. "That's what families do. But I'll start riding again, too, at some point, so you'll have to share."

"That won't be a problem, I guarantee it," I said, giving her a kiss on the cheek and then embracing her in a hug. "We might even get Patrick some lessons."

"We'll just be an equestrian family!" Mary exclaimed.

"What do you think about that, Pat?" I asked.

"I think you guys are *too* mushy!" he moaned, at which we gathered both kids into a group hug.

*Listen to your heart, and your dreams will follow.* I heard Mom's words rolling through my head.

THE days seemed to creep by until I could ride Dreamer again. I was updating our sales numbers late Wednesday afternoon when my cell phone rang.

"Hey, Mar," I answered. "How's it going?"

"Hi Jack, it's been a busy day. I'm sure yours has been too."

"Not too bad," I replied. "Numbers are looking up."

"That's good," she paused.

"Everything okay?"

"Everything's fine. I know you're busy, but I wanted to let you know that Annie called. She believes the farm is going up for sale in January."

"Oh, wow," I exhaled. It wasn't that the timing was surprising; it was just that hearing Mary say it with such assurance caught me off guard.

"How much?"

"She thinks it will list for $600,000."

I let out a little whistle.

"I know it's a lot," Mary conceded. "But, Jack, Annie has a good head start on the numbers . . . and I think this might be doable when we look at it."

"Alright, let's talk about it after we put the kids to bed."

"Okay, sounds good," Mary said, her excitement carrying through the cell signal. "I'll see you tonight."

"Okay, love you," I said as we ended the call.

The reality was that they were asking a lot of money for the farm, not an unreasonable amount, but it was still a lot of money. I sat back for a few minutes, daydreaming, imagining myself in a different life if it could all come together.

I have no idea how long I had been sitting there, lost in thought, but I was jolted out of my reverie by "Danny Boy," although the whistle was getting louder this time. Then, to my surprise, I looked up and saw Ed in the doorway.

"Happy Hump Day, Jack!" Ed grinned. "Never knew why they called it that . . . like each week was supposed to be some mountain to be climbed, and then we could just coast down the other side on Thursday and Friday."

"Well, I wouldn't mind coasting through to the weekend," I laughed. "Come in, Ed," I gestured. "If you have time, sit in my rarely used leather chair."

"An old man always has time, son, because he knows how precious it is."

"I know, here it comes. 'Don't blink,' right?" I raised my eyebrows.

"Not bad, Jack," he sank down on the chair with a sigh. "You beat me to my main point. You must have learned something."

"That I have, Ed, that I have."

"So, what's on your mind, Jack?"

"Is that your intuition asking?" I asked inquisitively.

"It's another byproduct of old age," he winked as he leaned back, ready to take in whatever I had to say. "I am a good listener, you know?" We were enjoying the friendly ribbing of a comfortable friendship.

"Annie called today and said she thinks the farm is going on the market in January. I can tell Mary is excited. She can hardly wait for me to get home to talk about it."

"Are you as excited as they are?"

"I am," I searched for the right words. "It's just that a lot would have to fall into place for us to consider it."

"Jack, let's back up a minute," Ed replied. "Have you asked yourself, 'What does Jack Kaneen want?'"

"Ed, I'm good at sales, and leading a team has been a natural progression for me; but, if I am being frank, it's a job that I have done well, a job that has been good to me. But I don't know if it's the life work people talk about doing every day because it's their passion and makes a real difference in the lives of others."

"Think back to some of our past conversations, Jack," Ed prodded. "What have you learned?"

"Well, I learned that it's the simple things that make a difference," I said, unsure if that was the answer Ed wanted.

"And what does that mean to you now? I think you have a pretty good idea."

I thought for a moment. "It's all about family, isn't it, Ed?"

"That's a big part of it," Ed concurred. "But, even more than that, to even get there, what has to happen?"

I sat there contemplating it, and then, like a wave that overtook me, it came to me instantly. "I have to be true to myself," I said. Then I repeated it with more assurance, "I have to be true to myself."

"Exactly," Ed said encouragingly. "Are you being true to yourself, Jack? I mean, does your work make you truly happy? Does it allow you to enjoy the simple things with your family that makes a difference in your life? Does it allow you to make a difference in the lives of those around you? And, if not, what would it look like to be true to yourself?"

Ed sat with me in the heavy silence.

"I can't give you the answer you're looking for, Jack," his voice caressed the air around me. "You're going to have to come to that on your own. But, take it from an old man, some people go through this life complacent, just getting by, never searching for meaning or purpose. You're searching, and you'll find it. I'm sure of it. You just have to ask yourself what you truly want . . . and then you have to listen for an answer." He stood up. "Well, it's time for this old fool to get to work." And, with that, he shuffled out the door.

*Old fool?* Ed was nothing of the sort. He was indeed a very wise, old man and one I was coming to like and admire more and more each time we spoke.

# CHAPTER SIXTEEN

# ADVOCATES

R EADY TO GO, CHAD?" I ASKED AS I PEEKED MY
head into his cubicle Thursday morning.

"Sure am," he responded. "I was just getting the prototypes
packed up. I'm excited. I really think he's going to like them. Thanks
again for suggesting this trip, Jack."

"Are you kidding? It's a team effort, and this is your baby. You
put a lot of time, energy, and brain power into this project. What you
have helped Dr. Waverly create will make a major difference in sales
for this company."

"No pressure, right, Jack?" Chad laughed as he closed the lid
on the plastic bin.

"No pressure," I replied.

It was clear and brisk, making it a great day to travel. Before we
got on the interstate, I pulled into a Dunkin' drive-thru. I knew how
Chad drank his coffee, so I ordered. "I'll take two medium coffees,
one with two creams and two sugars, and one with one cream and
one sugar."

"Please drive up," the voice said through the speaker.

"Thanks, Jack," Chad said, "I could use another cup this
morning."

"Me too," I replied. "Nothing like a Dunkin' on a cold
morning."

"Amen to that," Chad agreed.

Once we had our steaming cups, we each took a cautious sip.

Chad tended to be a quiet guy, but as I pulled onto the interstate, he seemed more silent than usual. "So, what's going on in your world, Chad?" I asked. "We haven't really had too much time to talk lately."

"You're a busy man, Jack, always on the road and working hard."

"Chad, let's be fair," I replied just as quickly, "you work equally as hard, just in a different capacity. I could never do what you do."

"But I got to tell you, Jack, sometimes it does feel like the same ol' thing, different day."

"What do you mean?" I could tell by his voice that there was more to the story.

"Oh, I don't know," Chad replied, watching the world pass by the window as we drove on. "I feel like I have more to offer like I'm unable to live up to my full potential."

"I think I understand what you mean," I responded, hoping it would encourage him to keep talking.

"Jack, our jobs are so different, and I don't think for a minute that I would want your job either," Chad seemed to be trying to assure me. "You've heard the old slogan, 'Join the Navy and see the world through a porthole'?"

"I have," I said, prompting him to continue.

"Well, I'm an engineer seeing the world through my cubicle."

"That makes sense," I affirmed. "I'm really sorry you feel that confinement, Chad. This has been a challenging year for all departments."

"You can say that again," Chad nodded. "I know Bill is on you a lot for numbers, but he is relentless about project timelines too. Sometimes he checks in multiple times about the same issue even before a deliverable is due . . . like I can't function on my own," he said with more than a hint of sarcasm. Then I saw a look of fear or regret, or both, dart across his face.

"Chad, please know that our conversation stays with us. You and I have built a lot of trust."

"This conversation stays here?" he asked hesitantly.

"Of course, Chad," I confirmed. "Anything you want to share between us stays just between us."

"I really appreciate that, Jack. Life just seems to get so complicated. My wife and I both work, and, most of the time, we're too tired to talk when we get home, so we put on the television and look for a show or a movie or just watch late-night talk shows and end up falling asleep."

"I can relate," I confessed. We both took a couple long sips of our coffees, and I thought about how Chad was on the same hamster wheel Ed talked about. I could sense it.

"I can't begin to tell you I have a fraction of the answers," I broke into the silence, "but I can tell you I have come to some new understandings lately. I don't know if you've noticed, but I haven't been staying as late at the office as I used to."

"I just figured you were dining with clients."

"There are some lessons I've learned over the last few weeks, truths I guess I always knew but was never open to accepting."

"What lessons?" Chad asked, and I could see that he was sincerely interested.

"First, it's the simple things that make a difference."

"But nothing seems simple anymore, at least not since shortly after that night when I showed you the instruments on Solidworks."

"What's changed?" I asked.

"There has been such a push to get these instruments out that the stress just suddenly piled up. I couldn't let the company down. I couldn't let you and the sales team down."

"Chad, you have never let us down, and what you do is seriously underappreciated."

"Thank you for saying that, Jack," Chad replied sincerely while lifting his coffee for another sip. "Almost cool enough to drink," he chuckled, and I took a long sip too.

"Fact is, Chad, stress and this hamster wheel of success can make you lose sight of the simple things. I used to think exactly what you said, that nothing is simple anymore. But, with the help of a wise friend, I realized that it's the simple things that are important to the people you care about and who care about you." I paused again for a sip of coffee. "Chad, I bet if you went for a walk with your wife when you got home or did something you used to do when you first met, you would see a difference. Actually," I paused, "I'll go one step further: you will *feel* a difference."

"Huh," he seemed lost in thought. "You just made me think of how much we used to like to hike."

"There you go," I lifted my Dunkin' cup in a toast. "You came up with that in two seconds. You need to take a minute to breathe and celebrate your accomplishment. It's about being mindful enough to be present. Believe me, your wife will enjoy being with the old Chad."

"Okay, Jack, I'll give it a try this weekend. But you said there were truths . . . plural."

"Well, Chad, I'm not saying I have it all figured out yet, but there are a couple more lessons I've learned."

"And, they are?"

"Well, the second is to be true to who you are. I understand now that if you take time to appreciate the simple things with the people who care about you, wheels are set in motion. You begin to be more open to new ideas. Someone told me it's like when you are driving along, and someone tells you to look for red cars. Next thing you know, the highway is filled with them because subconsciously, you are looking for them."

"Like that one right there?" Chad pointed. "And that one right there?"

"And that one right there," I laughed, glad he got the point I was trying to make.

"Okay, I get that," Chad nodded. "But what exactly does it mean to be true to who you are?"

"For me, being true to myself means not losing sight of who I am and where I came from. It's staying true to my values and being present enough to know what's important to me, my family, and others who care about me."

"Wow! I just thought you were another sales guy," Chad mused. "You're quite the philosopher."

"No," I chuckled, "I'm afraid I'm just a student trying to find my way, making sure I know what's in my heart. The same wise friend said my dreams will follow if I listen to my heart."

I could see that I had given Chad a lot to think about, so I let that sink in for a few minutes as I reflected on what he had said earlier. "Chad, you said you feel like you are not living up to your full potential."

"Did I say that?" he replied, attempting to downplay his earlier comment.

"You did," I confirmed. "In my book, that means you're constantly trying to get better, which is good."

"Jack, I don't really have this type of conversation with anyone."

"Well, if everyone needs one thing, it's a small group of advocates in life."

"Advocates?"

"People you trust. They are the ones who will give it to you straight. They will pick you up when you're down . . . or give you a good, swift kick in the derriere when you need it. They will steer you clear of the 'misery loves company' crowd, especially when things aren't going so well, or the stress piles up like you said."

*Are these things coming out of Jack Kaneen's mouth?* I thought to myself. I knew Chad was a good person with a big heart, and I also knew that if I could say just one thing to help him, to pay it forward, I wanted to be his advocate. I found myself thinking back through my recent conversations with Ed. I realized it was easy to talk about all this with Chad because I was internalizing what I had been learning over the past month or so.

"You see, Chad," I broke into the silence once again, "if you are mindful enough to be present in the moment, it's going to lead you to ask yourself some important questions."

"Like what?"

"Well, let me ask you a question I've recently asked: what would be your dream job? I mean, if you could do anything for a living, what would it be? Not just a job, but your life's work, something that leaves you fulfilled and allows you to leave a legacy?"

"So that's actually an easy one. I would own my own manufacturing business."

"Really?" I was somewhat surprised by how quickly he answered. "What type of manufacturing business?"

"We're all familiar with 3D printing, but I think the demand will far exceed what the industry can handle."

"Wait a minute, you mean 3D printing of implants? Companies are doing that now."

"They are, Jack. But, take US Ortho for instance," he suggested, "all of our stuff is forged and machined. We can't just convert our manufacturing overnight. And the big guys are so invested in their current manufacturing methods, it will take them years to convert."

"Sounds like you have given this a lot of thought."

"I have," Chad nodded. "And I think that if I could get one or two big customers . . . Who knows? Someday the company could even get acquired."

We were nearing Delaware, and I could see the traffic picking up as we pulled off the exit. But, glancing at the clock on the dash, I could see we were still ahead of schedule. Thankfully, we left early; otherwise, we would surely be late. Traffic in this area could be bad. Add just one fender bender, and you wish you would have packed a lunch.

"Remember what I said a few minutes ago? If you listen to your heart, and your dreams will follow."

"I really like that saying."

"Well, Chad, I have been on a hamster wheel chasing success. When you do that, you miss a lot. I've realized that, and I'm making changes."

"I welcome your insight, Jack. I know you better now than in all the years we have worked at the company."

"The feeling is mutual, my friend. You have so much potential. Please call me if you ever need anyone to bounce some things off of. I don't have all the answers, but I will be your advocate and an ear to listen."

"Thanks, Jack."

"Now," I paused for effect, "What will you do this evening when you get home?"

"Do you have to ask?" he laughed. "I'm going to talk my wife into going for a walk and plan to go on a day hike this weekend."

"Good for you, good for you!"

By that time, we were just about to enter the parking lot of Delaware Orthopedics.

"We kind of lost track of time talking, Jack," Chad said,

sounding slightly nervous. "Should we go over some things before we go in?"

"Chad, I have known Dr. Waverly for a long time; he has met you through Zoom calls, and the two of you have had countless calls and email exchanges. So just relax, be yourself, and follow my lead. Chuck will be glad to see you. Our goal in this meeting is to make Chuck feel like he has accomplished something here. With Chuck, it's always been about making a difference and leaving a legacy."

"Geez, you know him that well?" Chad asked incredulously.

"Sure do. While my job is sales, it is also establishing relationships; Chuck is just one of those guys I found common ground with."

"Hi, Kristi." Before I could get another word out, she said, "He's been waiting for you, Jack. What do you have for him that's so special? He's been acting like a little kid since he got here this morning."

"Kristi, this is our engineer, Chad Hanson. He designed the kinematic instruments with Dr. Waverly for his knee procedures, and we have them here for him today."

"Well, that explains it," Kristi nodded. "Nice to meet you, Chad. You're with a good guy here. We like to see Jack," she whispered, "but don't tell him that."

"You're too kind, Kristi. Chad is the one behind the scenes who really makes our company tick. I'm just along for the ride because I like coming here."

"Jack is just being modest, Kristi, but let's not build him up too much, or his head won't fit through the door," Chad joked, clearly more comfortable than when we first arrived.

"Follow me, guys," she said as she buzzed us through the door to the back office. "I'll put you in room one so you can set up, and I'll tell him you're waiting."

"No hurry," I replied.

Kristi left us in the silence of the exam room.

"Do you think he'll be long?" Chad whispered, laying the instruments on the exam table in a neat row.

I chuckled when Chad started whispering. "What about exam rooms makes us feel like we need to whisper like we're exchanging top secret information?"

"Who has top secret information?" Chuck bellowed as he pushed open the door.

I didn't even have time to intervene as the larger-than-life figure of Dr. Waverly descended upon Chad with a tight-gripped, Marine-style handshake. "You must be Chad Hanson! I have really been looking forward to meeting you in person. We have had so many calls; I feel like I know you."

"I know," Chad replied. "I feel the same way."

"What have you got for me here, Chad?"

"Well, these are the instruments, no more plastic prototypes," Chad smiled as he turned toward the table.

For a few silent minutes, Chad looked on in anticipation as Chuck studied the instruments intently, examining every guide, looking them up one side and then down the other for precision.

Finally, he looked up at Chad. "These are fantastic!" he exclaimed. "Chad, you have done an incredible job. Whatever they're paying you, it's not enough."

"Let me give you our CEO's phone number," Chad joked again, and I could read the relief on his face. "Seriously," Chad's manner changed, "you really like them?"

"Chad, I have worked with many companies over the years, and I can tell you no one has been such a pleasure to work with and produced such great quality instruments in the time you had to get this done. I can't thank you enough."

"That means a lot coming from you, Dr. Waverly."

"Next question," Chuck was on to the next item. "How many sets can I have, and when can I have them?"

For the first time, I felt compelled to jump in. "Chad has also done a great job with the build and the allocation. We have four sets for you ready to go that we can get down to you for next week's cases."

"Perfect! Let's take a minute and go over to my office." We followed Chuck down the hall.

"Have a seat," he motioned as he sat behind his desk.

"Jack, I have some good news for you. One of our surgeons has decided to move closer to his family on the West Coast."

"Okay, why is that such good news?"

"It's good news because my caseload is about to double." Then, turning to Chad, he added, "so, my newfound friend, that means we probably need a few more sets."

In unison, Chad and I almost shouted, "No problem!"

"Good," Chuck laughed. "I didn't think it would be."

"So, now that the business is out of the way, Jack, remember what we talked about last time you were here?"

"You mean the seminars?"

"No, we can talk about that again next time. I mean our talk about how it's the simple things that make a difference."

"Oh, yes, of course, I do." Seeing Chad from the corner of my eye, I could tell that his reaction was about the same as mine had been during that conversation Chuck was referencing.

"Well, I have decided to take that to heart. You guys will see a nice increase over the next year and a half, but I need to pay attention to the simple things. I'm not going to miss anything anymore."

"So, what are your plans?" I prodded.

"I will still work here, but I'm going to buy a place up in Boston to spend more time with my daughter and her family."

"That's great, Chuck!" I encouraged him.

"And you know what else, Jack? I may not have told you this, but I have always dreamed of building boats. We surgeons make plenty of money to buy big boats, but I have always dreamed of *building* them. So, I'm going to listen to this old heart and bet on the fact that my dreams will follow."

At this, I was just as taken aback as Chad, but by now, I had more practice keeping a good poker face when I found these life lessons shared repeatedly. "Now, Chuck," I grinned, "that's what I call being true to yourself."

"Yes, I guess you could call it that, Jack."

About that time, Kristi peaked in. "Doc, you have a patient in room three."

"I'll be right there."

With that, we all stood, and Chuck grabbed Chad's hand for another firm handshake.

"What's the matter, Chad? You okay?" Chuck had no doubt noticed the look of bewilderment on Chad's face and his clammy hands.

"I'm good," Chad insisted, "just too much coffee on the drive down made me a little jittery."

"Well, cut back on that stuff," Chuck laughed. "Jack had the same problem last time he was here."

"Will do," I answered for Chad as he excused himself to gather the instruments. I knew exactly why he looked like he had just seen a ghost. Chuck had reinforced, almost verbatim, what Chad and I discussed on the way down from Philly.

We each had our own roller coaster of emotions as we left the office and walked back out to the parking lot. I had not anticipated the much-needed business, but I also couldn't believe that Chuck was taking action on some of what we had talked about in our last visit.

"Jack, this is all good, but I have never had a stranger morning in all my life. This stuff just doesn't happen. Does it?"

"It happens, Chad," I gave him a hearty pat on the back. "It's been happening to me because I'm more present and open to what I may have missed before."

"Jack, I need to process all of this, but I can't thank you enough for allowing me to come with you today. This may really make a difference for me."

"Change takes time, Chad, but you are going to figure it out," I said as I unlocked the vehicle. "One thing I wanted you to see is just how much you are appreciated. You hit a home run with these instruments. You should be proud."

"Thank you again, Jack."

"It's a team effort. Now let's get home," I said while starting the engine. " That walk is going to do you good."

SATURDAY finally arrived, and we were back at the stables. While Mary helped Elizabeth and Patrick groom Sage, I was brushing Dreamer and filling Alissa in on the situation with the farm.

"Alissa, do you think it's a stretch to think we could revitalize an old farm and turn it into a successful business?"

"I like to think anything is possible if we put our minds to it," Alissa smiled. "And judging from your ride last week, I would say you definitely have the skills to make it happen. It is almost like riding a bike; you never forget."

"You never forget," I nodded. "And my legs won't let me forget either," I laughed, reaching down toward my right hamstring.

"That's true," Alissa agreed, "we don't bounce back like the kids. But seriously, you know business and horses. We would miss you for sure; but, hey, you never know when you may need another horse . . . or we would for that matter."

"That would be great," I agreed.

"Okay, Kaneen family," Alissa said, clapping her hands and heading to the indoor arena, "it's time to ride."

# CHAPTER SEVENTEEN

# DOWN TO THE WIRE

W E CLOSED OCTOBER AND NOVEMBER UP another three points in total. As the first week of December rolled in, we were sitting at 96 percent to quota, with the possibility of closing at 98 percent. But, of course, the team was still fighting for 98 or higher as it would put everyone in a position for a bonus. I was proud of them . . . but I also felt a bit like the coach whose team was still in the playoffs trying to get a shot at the Super Bowl.

I called our last meeting of the year for the first Thursday in December. I told everyone they could bring their spouse or significant other for our Christmas get-together. The winter weather cooperated, and everyone made it in on time. We got a room with a big table at Pat's on Wednesday evening. It was everyone's favorite, and we enjoyed an evening of pizza and some choice of wine or beer.

Just before we ate, I welcomed anyone who wanted to do so to join me in giving thanks to God for our meal and for a great year.

"Lord," I began, "thank You for bringing us all here this evening and for watching over us through the ups and downs of a turbulent year. You protected us, kept us safe, and guided us through difficult moments. Through Your grace, we have persevered and are better and stronger versions of ourselves. We thank You for bringing us all together and for this food we are about to receive, and we ask that you continue to guide us through the end of the year and throughout our lives. Amen."

"Amen," several people repeated in concert.

"Let's eat," I concluded, "it's time to celebrate!"

After enjoying some great pizza, everyone was standing around conversing in small groups of two or three. Mary and I made the rounds, thanking everyone again for being there.

David Anderson, Carol's husband, and I happened to be getting a glass of wine simultaneously.

"Jack," David said, "Carol sure thinks a lot of you. She sees you as a mentor, and I can see the difference your guidance has made in her this year."

"Thanks, David. Carol is a special person. If it were not for her persistence, we wouldn't be sitting where we are year to date."

"Well, Jack, she would tell you that she couldn't have done it without your support."

"David, if there is one thing I have learned, it is that when you earn people's trust, and that is a very sacred thing, they will do whatever it takes to accomplish the mission. Maybe that's a Marine thing, but I have found it true in whatever I have done as a leader."

"That's sound advice, Jack, and it shows in your people." David seemed like a great guy. Watching them together, I was thrilled that Carol seemed to have found a man who saw her for who she was worth and seemed capable of a mutually supportive relationship.

The evening had been sincerely enjoyable, and the drive home was peaceful, with the city lights and Christmas lights shimmering through the windows.

"Jack, I'm so proud of you," Mary said, interrupting Bing Crosby's version of "The Best Things in Life Are Free" from *It's a Wonderful Life* playing over the radio. "I spoke with everyone on the team as you were making the rounds, and each of them credits you with getting so close to quota this year."

"I couldn't be prouder of them, Mary. They could have panicked. They could have thrown in the towel. Take Pat, bouncing back from an illness to recapture his business when the competition was knocking at the door. And then there is Carol, not taking 'no' for an answer. I may have been at the helm, but even a ship pointed into the wind doesn't make headway without a good crew. It truly has been a team effort."

"You, my ever modest husband, have stayed the course," Mary patted my leg. "You don't build a great team without great leadership. Your team trusts you. You built that trust, and that's why the ship, as you say, is making headway."

"Well, we're not there yet. If we can get to 98 percent to quota, it will guarantee the team bonuses. But even then, I'm not sure the board will be satisfied. It's just the way they are."

"Well, if I were a betting girl, I'd have all my chips on you and your team."

"I love you, Mar. I couldn't do any of this without you."

"WOW!" I exclaimed as I entered the conference room. "Kathy, you are too much!"

Kathy was there before everyone the next morning. She had the audio-visual all setup, notepads around the table, festive Hershey kisses at everyone's place, fresh water, and a carafe of coffee in the center of the table.

"Jack, it's all in a morning's work," she laughed while walking by me. "I'll be right back. Just going to get my computer and a couple of folders."

I heard the elevator ding a few times over the next 20 minutes, and everyone made their way into the conference room.

Bill came in last, as usual, just as I started. But, instead of sitting at the head of the table, he sat in a chair in the corner of the room without a word. Everyone seemed a bit on edge, but Bill seemed content to listen to my presentation and take a few notes. Once we moved into team reports, he retired to his office.

Jeff went first, as solid and steady as always.

"Jeff, I tell you what," I laughed, "with your love of tennis metaphors and your record of success, I think I may have to start calling you Roger Federer!" The compliment hit its mark.

"Well, I'm just going to stick with a sports analogy," Chris said as he stood for his presentation. "If getting our approval in October was a goal, I'm going for the two-point conversion with surgeons having many cases scheduled before the end of the month!"

"Score!" Jeff and I yelled simultaneously, holding our arms up like goalposts.

"Alright then, Chris, if Jeff is Roger Federer, I may just have to nickname you Dick Butkus!" As a Patriots fan, Butkus was the only Chicago Bears player I knew who was actually from Chicago.

"Not the best nickname," Chris laughed, "but he was a heck of a linebacker, so I'll take it."

After Chris finished his entire report, we broke for lunch with Philly cheesesteaks and salads from Cleavers just a few blocks away. Just as I finished my sandwich, I heard the door to the conference room open to my left. I turned, expecting to see Bill stepping in for a quick reminder about quota for the team. Instead, however, a friendly face popped through the door's opening, to my pleasant surprise.

"Chad!" I exclaimed. "You nearly missed lunch."

"I can't stay," Chad looked slightly disappointed, "but I

wanted to remind you that Dr. Waverly is adding additional cases for the last few weeks of the year."

"Yes," I nodded, taking the last sip of my soda. "I forgot to report that to the team this morning."

"Speaking of cases," Jeff jumped in, "I'm going to need at least two sets of the new instruments for Dr. Jensen in Atlanta."

"I have 10 sets ready to go!" Chad smiled broadly like a proud papa. "Just stop by my cubicle before you leave this afternoon, and I'll make sure you get them."

"I'm going to need at least two as well for my trip to Texas next week," Pat said as he opened his laptop to pull up his presentation while everyone was disposing of their trash and recyclables. Once everyone was back in their seats, Pat started with the news that Dr. Johnson had his first observation scheduled for the following Monday with surgeons from the Dallas-Fort Worth metro area. And even better than that was knowing that Pat was feeling healthy enough to head down to Texas next week to take Dr. Johnson, Andy, and the surgeons to a debriefing dinner after the observation.

Carol started her report right around 2 p.m.

"Well, I see that we've saved the best for last," she grinned as she pulled up her first slide, which read, "MORE GOOD NEWS!"

"Not only did we get the Maine Medical account back in October, but three of the highest volume surgeons are coming over to us as well!" Her next slide showed the names of the three competitive surgeons with their volumes over the past year. We skimmed the stats, and all broke into applause.

"Carol," I declared, "this is outstanding! You really deserve this after all your hard work on that account."

Carol finished her presentation with about 15 minutes to spare.

"It seems like all of this is really coming together as we get down to the wire," Pat said as Carol took her seat.

"I couldn't agree more, Pat," I said as I rose from my seat. And with that, I wrapped up not only the meeting but the year. "Team, this is the last time we will be together as a group this year. I want to thank each of you for your effort over this past quarter. I am proud of you, not just of your performance as a team but of your personal growth as well. Together, we are building something we can all be proud of, and I can sense that. So, let's keep our focus for the last furlong and make it a picture-perfect finish."

The team grabbed snacks for the road, lingering near the thermal carafes to fill their to-go cups and say their holiday goodbyes. This was a good bunch, and, as a leader, I wanted success for them even more than they did, more than they would ever know.

Pat and Jeff headed over to Chad's cubicle while Carol and Chris headed for the elevator. Once everyone had cleared out of the conference room, I retired to my office. I began to pull my notes if Bill wanted a complete meeting summary.

I had only been working for about 10 minutes when my cell phone buzz interrupted my typing.

"Hey, Mar," I said as I picked up the phone.

"Hi Jack, how was the meeting?" Mary asked.

"Still not tracking 100 percent, but I couldn't be happier with the team and the meeting today."

"What did Bill have to say?"

"Oddly, he didn't say anything. Instead, he took notes while I was speaking and then left for his office a short time later, and that's the last we saw of him."

"That isn't like him," Mary commented.

"Yeah, I know," I brushed it off. "So, what's up?" I asked, eager to change the subject.

"Annie has finished the numbers and emailed them to us, so you can check your personal email when you have a chance to look them over."

"Okay, thanks for letting me know. I'll take a look as soon as I finish my meeting summary."

I tried to jump back into my report summary, but curiosity got the best of me. I couldn't think about anything else, so I opened Annie's email. Mary was right. Annie had done a lot of work. It looked like she had thought of everything: the cost of the feed, the number of boarders needed to break even, and the profit and loss projection for three years. It was all there. She even had numbers for an equine-assisted learning program.

We would need to sell our house here for the down payment, and it would take some additional money—money that could come from a bonus if we were to hit 98 percent.

*Could we really do it?* I asked myself. *Could our lives really change that drastically? Could I really take charge of my own destiny?* The questions bubbled to the surface like a bottle of champagne hidden away, waiting for the right moment to be opened.

The chime of an email coming in jolted me back to reality. Carol had emailed from the airport to say that each new surgeon had multiple cases booked with our products before the end of the year. Then, another one popped in before I could even close Carol's email. This one was from Pat, saying Dr. Johnson added two additional cases.

Amazing what can happen when salespeople are excited about a product.

We had about two weeks left before business started winding down for the holidays, and this was one of those times when every unit counted. But, whatever happened, I felt like we were leaving nothing on the table.

With the summary complete and an email sent to Bill for review, I began to shut everything down for the night.

I smiled because, as if the song could read my mind, "Danny

Boy" came wafting down the hall. As it had once before, the tune seemed to grow louder as it got to the part about sunshine or shadow.

When I looked up, there stood Ed in my doorway. But instead of his usual mop, he held a cup of hot tea in each hand.

"Well, here's a surprise," he said in jest, "Jack Kaneen working late again."

"You brought me tea!" I exclaimed. "Now that *is* a surprise."

"I thought you might enjoy something warm before you head out into the cold," he handed me one cup and settled into the leather chair. "You look tired, Jack."

"Long meeting today."

"Yeah, I know."

We simultaneously took sips of the earthy liquid that held just the right amount of milk and honey.

"I heard a couple of your team members talking earlier about what a good leader you are."

"Really?" I asked in surprise.

"I came in a little earlier this afternoon to fill in for Gary on the fifth floor because his wife had surgery today. Unfortunately, I had to come up here first because I had left my feather duster in that empty cubicle yesterday. As I rode down the elevator, a woman and man talked about your meeting. They said that, while you didn't always agree, you were always doing what you thought was best for them."

"Wow," I took a deep, cleansing breath. "That's good to hear. I couldn't be happier with the team . . ."

"But?" Ed probed in a non-threatening way like he had a tendency to do. "I can tell something's weighing on you."

"But," I shook my head, "Bill came in for less than an hour, sat in the back of the room taking notes, and didn't even say a word. It was . . . odd, to say the least."

"Didn't you tell me recently that Bill and the board had backed off a bit this quarter?"

"They've hardly made a peep, which is strange since they were tough on everyone up until the end of September."

"But you've said you are happy with your team's performance, right?"

"I am, I am," I confirmed. "We seemed to have turned the corner this fall in more ways than one. Among other successes, today's meeting brought some great news on an account we had lost and got back, and now it is growing."

"Well, that sounds like congratulations are in order, Jack."

"Oh, I didn't really have anything to do with it," I demurred. "Carol was on top of it the whole way."

"You're being modest, Jack. You're her mentor, right?"

"I guess you could say that."

"See what happens when you touch a life? The rewards come back in ways you never expect."

"I hope you're right, Ed," I sighed. "No matter how Bill or the board feels about our efforts, I know that my team has done the very best they could. I feel like I have been able to really connect with them like never before. Of course, we've struggled, but we also have shared goals and a vision and have built mutual respect that I haven't felt since my Marine Corps days."

"That's the best attitude to take, Jack. You have persevered, and you have the trust of your team; no matter what happens, you can be at peace with that."

"Peace sounds good right about now," I admitted.

We both took another warm, comforting sip of tea.

"Annie sent us all her calculations today," I broke into the comfortable silence.

"So, is it doable, Jack?" Ed's eyebrows rose in anticipation of my response.

"I think it might be, Ed, I think it might be," I nodded. "But a lot would have to fall into place."

"You said that the last time we talked about the farm."

"Did I?" I asked.

"You did," Ed nodded. "Jack, do you remember a question I asked you during that conversation?"

"You ask a lot of questions, Ed."

We both chuckled.

"This was something I said you would have to figure out for yourself," he specified, "something you would have to ask yourself and then listen for the answer."

"You said I had to ask myself what I really want."

"And have you heard an answer yet, Jack?"

"Honestly, Ed, I'm not sure," I ran my forefinger around the rim of my cup as I gathered my thoughts. "But I realize that I could make a difference working with horses. I could do the training, but, even more importantly, I could develop a program that would not only introduce people to the horses but work with the horses as coaches in a way that could benefit leaders and their teams."

Ed seemed to analyze my response.

"Would it make you happy?" he prodded further.

"I really think it would."

"Would that allow you to enjoy the simple things in life with your family?"

"It absolutely would," I said without hesitation.

"Would it allow you to make a difference in the lives of those you touch?"

"I believe it would."

With that, Ed stood up, empty cup in hand. I stood too. He took a couple of steps toward me, reached across the desk, put his hand gently on my shoulder, and paused for a brief moment.

"You see, Jack, true riches lie in making a difference in people's lives. Giving back is not just about money; it's about discovering the possibilities in life. Sometimes all you need is a little nudge. You may never know the difference you made, but it will be there. That difference will appear, carried forward from generation to generation, like a wheel set in motion.

"Jack, I have no doubt you will hit your numbers," he said, "and I also have no doubt you will find your way to the next exciting chapter of your life, making a difference along the way."

"What makes you so sure?" I asked.

"I believe in you, son," he smiled.

When Ed finally removed his hand from my shoulder, he picked up my empty cup and headed out the door. At the doorway, he turned back.

"Take it from an old man, Jack; what it comes down to is this: listen to your heart, and your dreams will follow."

WHEN I returned downstairs after tucking Patrick and Elizabeth into bed, Mary had her laptop open on the kitchen table.

"Were you able to take a look at Annie's email?" she asked as I pulled a chair up next to her so we could both look at the numbers.

"I did," I acknowledged. "And, like Annie has always done, she did her homework. Did you help her out with the financials?"

"I *am* an accountant, you know?"

"I know, I know," I put my hand on hers. "I wasn't being facetious. What Annie sent is very thorough and detailed. But I want to know what *you* really think?"

"Well, Jack, I think it's entirely possible," she paused. "We owe about $200,000 on our mortgage, so we would have to get top dollar for this house. I would keep my job and work from home. I would just need to travel to the office for two days at the end of the quarter. Annie could help with the kids, so I don't see a problem." She paused again. "But you would need to hit your bonus. And the old post and beam barn will need a lot of work . . ."

"And we will *have* to build the indoor arena Annie proposed," I continued her train of thought. "With the winters up there, there is just no way we could sustain the business through the winter months without it."

"There's a lot to think about for sure," she nodded. "So much would have to fall into place."

I couldn't tell if she sounded hesitant or hopeful.

"Mar, I'm being drawn to this for reasons I'm not even sure I can explain."

"What was it that Annie said back at the cabin about listening to your heart?"

"Listen to your heart, and your dreams will follow."

"She said your mom used to say that."

"She did," I paused again. "Ed said the same thing this evening when I spoke with him."

"Ed, your janitor friend?"

"Yeah, it's funny how he just shows up at the right times."

"Well, Jack, maybe we all need a janitor in our lives."

"Maybe so," I replied. "He does make me think, and he helps me weed through all the garbage that collects in my head, that's for sure."

ONCE again, I felt like Saturday couldn't arrive soon enough. It was cold at the barn, and with the last few weeks of the year winding down, the horses' winter coats were as thick as they would be all year. While Alissa and Elizabeth were having their lesson, I had an opportunity to talk to Donna. Alissa had already informed her about our prospects with the farm. She advised me to ensure we would be filling an unmet need in that area and that we would be able to attract students for lessons and horses to board. I shared some numbers that Annie and Mary had pulled together, and she agreed that it sounded promising. I wasn't exactly surprised that Donna was familiar with equine-assisted learning. Still, I was a little taken aback when she said she had been looking into it as something they should consider at some point.

"Maybe you could come back here and do a course for us occasionally," she proposed. I couldn't help but feel that it sounded like we were moving closer and closer toward a sustainable business plan.

~

# CHAPTER EIGHTEEN

# A TIME TO BELIEVE

I T WAS THE FRIDAY BEFORE CHRISTMAS, AND AS I shut down my computer and gathered my things, Bill came in with his coat and scarf.

"Jack, I'm headed out tomorrow morning, taking the girlfriend up to Stowe Mountain, so I won't see you next week. I'll still be watching the numbers, of course, but I wanted to give you a head's up that there is going to be a board meeting on Wednesday, January 2nd, at 9 a.m. So I need you here."

"Okay, what is the meeting about?" I asked somewhat hesitantly.

"I can't give you a lot of details, and there's not much to prepare for in advance, but be ready to summarize the year for your team in case they have questions."

It was rare that I would be invited to a board meeting, so the thought made me more than a little nervous. But before I could get another question in, Bill turned on his heels and headed toward the elevator.

"Merry Christmas," he called back.

"Merry Christmas," I called after him, standing there behind my desk wondering if this was a good sign . . . or a bad sign.

I pulled on my coat, grabbed my trusty LL Bean bag, and shut off my light, but instead of walking toward the elevator, I turned toward the cubicles on the far left. I didn't hear the familiar whistle, and there was no sign of Ed. I even passed the break room on my way back to the elevator. No Ed. No "Danny Boy."

Ironically, a different song played over the speaker in the elevator, Andy Williams' "It's the Most Wonderful Time of the Year." And yet, rather than visions of candy canes, I found increasingly negative scenarios marching through my mind. As the elevator descended, so, it seemed, did my spirits.

*I need to talk to someone,* I thought to myself as I made my way to the parking garage. *I don't want to get home and dump this all on Mary.*

In the car, I cranked up the heat and hit speed dial.

"Jack, ol buddy!" Steve exclaimed as he answered the call. "How are you doing?"

"Cold," I laughed, "How are you?"

I wanted to wish him a 'Merry Christmas,' and I knew that he would understand, perhaps better than anyone, how I felt after the announcement Bill had sprung on me.

"I'm headed home for the weekend," Steve replied. "How about you?"

"Just pulling out of the parking garage."

We caught up as I drove the familiar streets back to the house. The voice of a friend and the soft glow of Christmas lights brightened my mood.

"So, how are your end-of-year numbers looking?" he asked the inevitable question.

"Well, Bill just dropped by and told me he wanted me to attend a board meeting on January 2nd."

"That's great!" Steve replied enthusiastically.

"Yeah?" I intended it to be a statement, but it came out as more of a question.

"Why would it be anything but?"

"Well, for starters, we aren't going to make quota."

"How can you be so sure?"

"Steve, you know me. I crunch the numbers every day."

"Quota isn't everything, Jack."

"It sometimes seems that way with this company," I stated matter-of-factly.

"So, you're worried?" Steve asked.

"I'm wondering if I will have a job going into the new year or if they are secretly making other plans," I answered him honestly. "I know it probably sounds like a stretch, but you know how it can be in this business, Steve. Remember what happened with DeWitt Marcus? Sometimes, if they think someone is better connected and can bring a boatload of business, they'll make a change. Sometimes it just doesn't matter whether you're 96 percent to quota, 98 percent to quota, or 100 percent."

"Well, I don't think you should overreact, but I know you're right. Unfortunately, job stability in this industry can be unpredictable at best."

"And another thing that's been on my mind," I continued, "we have the opportunity to purchase back our family farm."

"Wow," exclaimed Steve, "talk about timing. Maybe it's good that you and Mary are considering the farm in case you may need a backup plan."

"That's just it, Steve. The farm is turning into more than a backup plan, but I really need to keep my job while we make some critical decisions. I can't afford to lose my salary before we sell the house. We would never get approval for another loan to buy the farm. And it's not just me; I worry about the team. None of them can afford to lose their jobs, or deserves to, for that matter."

"Jack, you have put the full-court press on everyone, and you've done it professionally, as far as I can see," Steve reminded me in a reassuring tone. "And you said you are satisfied with your team's performance."

"I am," I said. "The team has done everything to put us in a position to finish as strong as possible."

"Well, who's to say that Bill and the board don't see this last quarter exactly the same way you do?"

"You know, you're right, Steve," I let out a deep breath. "I knew you would help me refocus."

"Hey, that's what advocates do for each other, right, Jack? You've certainly done the same for me a time or two. Look, I'm just about home, and I'm sure you are too. How about we both just enjoy celebrating the holidays with our families."

"It's the simple things that make the difference," I repeated what had become a mantra.

"Now, who's offering the advice?" Steve laughed.

"Oh, that's not my wisdom. That's from my friend Ed."

"Ed? The janitor?"

"The one and only."

"Sounds like we could all use a janitor in our lives, Jack."

"I think we could, Steve. We all should have an Ed in our lives. Merry Christmas to you and your family."

"Give my love to Mary and the kids," Steve returned. "And make sure you let me know how that meeting goes on the 2nd."

THE office was quiet on Christmas Eve. Knowing Bill would be out, I had told Kathy to take the day off to spend with her girls, and it appeared that more than half the staff had done the same.

It was snowing heavily by early afternoon, and everything

city-wide seemed to shut down early. I was anxious to get home and watch Christmas movies with the family.

"See you, Wednesday, Jack," Chad stopped in my doorway as he buttoned his coat. "I promised my wife I would only come in for half the day."

"Good for you," I smiled. "I'm just about to head out myself. I was just hoping I could catch Ed before I leave. You haven't seen him, have you?"

"Ed?"

"You know, the janitor," I explained.

"Um, no," Chad seemed puzzled. "I haven't seen him."

"Okay, well, drive safe. It looks like it's really coming down out there."

"I will," he replied, "and make sure you do the same."

"I hope you and your wife have a wonderful Christmas, Chad," I said as he headed for the elevator.

"Merry Christmas, Jack," he called back.

I switched off my computer, pushed my chair back from my desk, and walked to my windows. The street below looked like a winter wonderland, with people bustling to get home in the swirling snow.

I couldn't help but ask myself, *Is this all there is? What happens after the year is over?* The answer was self-evident. We start at zero, and we do it all again. While I knew there was a sense of accomplishment in all of that, I had to ask myself if it was enough.

Grabbing my coat and bag, I took a quick walk around the cubicles; but just like Friday night, I was disappointed to find no sign of Ed.

Just then, I heard the elevator ding. I walked quickly to catch it, but I must have been too slow because the doors closed as I rounded the corner. Then, suddenly, the doors reopened, and there stood Ed, a dark coat over his work clothes and a red scarf at his neck.

"Going my way?" he smiled.

"Yes, sir," I said cheerfully as I stepped into the car while he held the doors open. "I was hoping I would see you today. I wanted to wish you a Merry Christmas."

"Now, whatever would make you think of this old, white-haired man on Christmas Eve?" he asked, his deep chuckle sounding remarkably like a "Ho! Ho! Ho!" as he rubbed his white beard.

"So, what are your plans for Christmas?" I asked Ed as we started our descent.

"Well, I needed to drop something off here, and for the rest of the day, I'll be enjoying all the simple things that make the difference, Jack," he winked. "What about you? When do you have to come back to work?"

"Well, I just found out Friday night that the board has called a meeting for Wednesday morning, January 2nd," I said, "and they want me there."

"Wow, what do you think that's all about?" Ed asked, and I could tell he was trying to read my face.

"Well," I replied, "it's either good news or bad news."

"You think it could be bad news, Jack?" he asked, looking at me quizzically.

"Well, I'll just say that they hadn't included me in meetings in the past when we met our quota."

"Your team rallied this quarter, didn't they?" Ed asked. "You said you were proud of them."

"They did," I nodded, "and I am. But we didn't make 100 percent to quota."

"Well, that may be, Jack," Ed conceded, "but quota isn't everything."

"You're right, Ed," I said. "I am thankful to you for helping me recognize that. I feel like I have been able to really connect with my team like never before. Of course, we've struggled, but we also have shared goals and a vision and have built mutual respect that I haven't felt since my Marine Corps days."

"Things will happen as they are supposed to, Jack. You just have to believe."

"Now you really do sound like Santa . . . or Clarence, the angel from *It's a Wonderful Life*."

I noticed the elevator ding as we passed the 10th floor.

"Jack, it's clear from our recent conversations that you know what you want, so I just have one more question for you."

"What is that?" I asked.

"Why do you want it?"

"Why?" I repeated, buying myself a few seconds to think. "Well, as I've said, I want to work with horses . . ."

"But why?" Ed rarely interrupted me, but he seemed so intent on ensuring I understood what he was getting at. "You see, Jack, once you find the answer, the why will lead you directly to your purpose, and once you have that, you can walk confidently into the future."

As if on cue, we reached the first floor, and the doors opened to the lobby. As we walked out, I wasn't necessarily confident about my future, but I was sure I didn't want our conversation to end.

"So, why would you consider leaving your job and moving your family to work with horses?" Ed repeated his question to me in more specific terms. Though I had no idea the answer he was trying to guide me toward, I was glad he wanted to continue our discussion. We stood near the front glass doors, watching the snow falling steadily.

"I want to do it because I believe I can make a difference in people's lives," I answered earnestly.

"What kind of difference, Jack?"

"Discerning destiny," I said almost to myself.

"What was that?" Ed asked, leaning in a little to hear better.

"I said 'discerning destiny.' The words just came to me. I think that the root of why I want to pursue equine-assisted learning is to help people determine their true destinies."

"Okay, you want to help people find their true destinies. That sounds good," Ed nodded. "But what will that do?"

"You aren't going to make this easy for me, are you?"

"Nothing worthwhile is ever easy, Jack." Ed's voice at this point might have sounded stern had anyone else been in the lobby. Still, his eyes were filled with such sincere interest he looked as if he were verging on the brink of some great discovery.

"If I can help people experience being present enough to begin asking themselves the right questions," I searched for the right words, "then their dreams will follow and become a reality because it is in our moments of decision that our destiny is shaped."

"And there you have it, Jack. That is your purpose!"

"Discerning destiny," I repeated the words, running them over in my mind.

"Jack, you have come to a place where fear can't conquer you anymore."

"Why is that?" I asked.

"Because, my friend, the power of purpose will always rise above fear, allowing you to accomplish your mission. You will open thousands of people's hearts and minds along the way. When people find their purpose, and when they decide at that moment to pursue it, whether they realize it or not, they have taken the first step toward creating a bright, new future—a new destiny."

"Discerning destiny," I repeated again; this time, it felt more comfortable on my tongue.

Ed pulled a hat out of his coat pocket like the cabby had worn in Dallas and positioned it on his white head. Then, he pulled a pair of gloves that matched his scarf out of his other pocket and began pulling them on. I did the same.

"Jack, this has been a year of transition for you. But, the year that is coming is bringing new beginnings. I can feel it." He sounded almost like a soothsayer, like the Spirit of Christmas Yet to Come . . . only much friendlier and bearing much better news.

He pushed open the glass door, and I followed him out of the office building.

I asked Ed if he was going to be okay getting home.

"It will take more than snow to worry this old soul," he said confidently. "I don't have far to go."

"Ed, I don't know why you came into my life when you did, but you have opened my mind and encouraged me to consider possibilities and to never settle for less than I can be. I'll never forget it."

"Jack, it's been a pleasure getting to know you. I'm proud of you. In my travels past and in my travels yet to come, I will never find a better student and a better friend."

"Merry Christmas, Ed," I reached out my gloved hand to shake his, and he pulled me into a hug.

"Merry Christmas to you," he said.

With that, my friend turned down the street, and I walked through the snow to the parking garage. I thought to myself that this had possibly been the most enlightening and powerful conversation I had ever had. I looked back, thinking I would wave a final goodbye, but the snow had already cut visibility to a point where even his red scarf had seemingly disappeared into thin air. I was overcome by the strange feeling that he had just said goodbye for good. I brushed the feeling aside with the snow on my shoulder, hoping he would be safe.

AS I let myself in at home, the sounds of Christmas music playing and the aroma of freshly baked Christmas cookies filled the air. Mary was just putting the traditional white frosted cake in the center of the table. It read simply, "Happy Birthday, Jesus!"

"It's good to have you home," Mary greeted me with a hug.

Before I could ask where Elizabeth and Patrick were, they ran into the kitchen with exuberant cries of, "Daddy, you're home!"

After an early dinner, Patrick helped me light a fire in the fireplace. Mary brought a plate of Christmas cookies in and placed it on the coffee table. Elizabeth brought in a smaller plate of cookies for Santa. While I put them on the mantle to make sure Brady wouldn't get into them when we weren't paying attention, Elizabeth returned with a glass of milk. Patrick followed behind her with hot chocolate for his sister and him. Mary handed me a cup of festive eggnog sprinkled with nutmeg.

The kids couldn't wait for us to turn on *Santa Claus is Coming to Town*. They were fast asleep when we were halfway through *It's A Wonderful Life*. I carried Elizabeth up first and tucked her in. As I was carrying Patrick up the stairs, he had woken up at some point, but I knew he was faking being asleep. As I pulled the covers up to his chin, he opened one eye and squinted at me. "Tricked you, Dad," he said, "I was awake."

"Well, you won't trick Santa," I tweaked his nose, "so you better get to sleep if you want him to come tonight."

"I will, Dad," he said, closing his eyes tight.

"Good night, Pat. I love you."

"Love you, too, Dad."

By the time I joined Mary back on the sofa, she had brewed us each a cup of hot tea, and, knowing that with my sweet tooth, I had been eyeing that frosted cake since I walked in the door, she had sliced us each a piece.

"Mar, this has been quite a year."

"How so?" Mary asked.

"Well, here we are considering the possibility of a big move. A year ago, who would have even thought that we would be considering buying the old farm, moving to a different state, and starting a business?"

" Jack, I think God has a way of sending us His help and guidance to move us in certain directions."

I told Mary about my conversation with Ed while leaving the office.

"Maybe your janitor is another Clarence from *It's a Wonderful Life*," she grinned, the firelight twinkling in her eye.

"It's amazing the conversations I have had with him over these last several months. He just has a way of asking thought-provoking questions at the right time. He has allowed me to see what I had been missing right before me."

"I can see the change," Mary acknowledged. "Jack, you have been a different person. Well, not different. It's like I have the old Jack back. Not that you were ever gone, but you seem so present lately like you've become focused on what's most important to you."

"I feel like I have found a sense of peace in knowing that I have done the very best I can do," I said sincerely, "a satisfaction in knowing that I have invested into the lives of those around me. And I know that is more lasting than any quota or bonus. I think the old Jack would be stressed about the meeting next week."

"I still don't think keeping you in suspense about this meeting over the holidays is fair."

"That's just the way Bill operates. I think that, in his mind, he is doing right by everyone. He doesn't consider anyone else's perspective or weigh long-term repercussions beyond profit margin."

"Sounds like Bill could use a good talk with the janitor," Mary replied.

"I would have to agree with that," I laughed.

"We did say that everyone should have a janitor, right?" she laughed with me.

"We did," I agreed. "But seriously, we all need good advocates in life to shock us back into reality—people like Ed . . . and Annie . . . and you." I put my arm around Mary and pulled her close. "I know I've said this before, but I really couldn't do any of this without you and Patrick and Elizabeth . . . oh, and I can't forget Brady," I grinned as I ruffled the fur on his head where it lay in my lap.

"Well, let's hope the meeting is all positive, Jack," Mary said as she laid her head on my shoulder. "You have given your best to this company. I don't see how it could be anything less."

"You know, Mary, it doesn't really matter tonight. Christmas is a time to be thankful for all we have and trust Him with what is to come."

"You're right, Jack. We have a lot to be thankful for." Mary reflected, "especially compared to so many other people."

"It's a good reminder to pray for everyone struggling," I added.

"I believe God has a plan," she said as she nestled closer. "We just have to be present enough to realize it."

"I believe He does, Mar, I believe he does." I kissed her on the forehead. "And isn't that what Christmas is? It's a time of magic—a time to believe."

## CHAPTER NINETEEN

~

# NEW BEGINNINGS

NEW YEAR'S DAY HAD COME AND GONE IN THE blink of an eye. Here it was, 10 p.m. on Tuesday, January 1st already. A new year. What would this year bring? Ed had said that the past year has been a year of transition and that this year will be a year of new beginnings.

With Mary upstairs reading and Patrick and Elizabeth fast asleep in their beds, I sat in the silence of the evening, interrupted only by the occasional drop of ice in the ice maker, thinking about how lucky I was. Brady, who lay sound asleep on my lap, couldn't care less about my musings. Life was great for him as long as he had his family around him and my lap to lay his head on at the end of a long day. *The life of a dog,* I thought to myself.

I had always thought that we were free to think and believe as we wanted as individuals. I couldn't help but know that God had a plan, and I found comfort in that. I had confidence that everything would work out the way it was supposed to, so I had no more trepidation going into tomorrow's meeting. If they wanted to replace me, that was fine. With Ed's help, I found my purpose and was comforted knowing that my team and I had done our best.

With that, I shut off the living room light, and Brady followed me quietly up the stairs. We were ready to sleep our way into whatever the new year held in store for us.

I got to the office at about 7 a.m. I fired up the laptop and reviewed the numbers for the final time: 97.6 percent to quota. The team had made their bonuses. I couldn't have been happier, considering everything we had to overcome. As for me, I had no idea what the board was thinking, not having made their cherished 100 percent.

"Happy New Year!" Kathy's exuberant greeting startled me halfway out of my chair.

"Happy New Year!" I had been deep in thought, contemplating the board meeting.

"I'm sorry, Jack, did I startle you?"

"It's okay, Kathy. I needed to get the blood flowing anyway."

"Well, here's a fresh cup of coffee to help with that," she smiled, placing the cup on my desk. "Oh, before I forget, there was a letter for you," she paused as she shuffled through the folders in her hand. "Here it is." She handed me the plain white envelope.

As Kathy left, I inspected the envelope on all sides. All it said was "To Jack." Almost instantly, I had a feeling it was from Ed. As I opened the letter and unfolded the paper, I sat back and began to read:

*Dear Jack,*

*I apologize that you are reading this in a letter instead of hearing it from me in person. Unfortunately, I'm not good at goodbyes. I don't think I will ever be, and that's a flaw.*

*I know this is an important day for you, so I wanted to be here with you, if only in my words.*

*You, Jack Kaneen, are a rare individual. You have been a good student. You have come so far in just a few months and have found your purpose. First, you asked yourself what you wanted and why you wanted it, and now that you know, it will make all the difference. You will help others discern their destinies, open the hearts and minds of countless people—more than you will ever know—and, in so doing, leave a lasting legacy. I know your life and journey from this point forward are just beginning and will be filled with possibilities.*

*Don't ever look in the rearview mirror. Remember, the windshield is much bigger because what's in front matters most. Never lose sight of the simple things that make all the difference, and stay true to yourself.*

*Today you will be challenged and need to make some decisions. Remember what it is you want . . . and why you want it. Don't lose sight of your purpose.*

*Don't worry about me. I believe our paths will cross again, God willing. In the meantime, when you think of me, drop a line in the pond on a clear, cool morning when the mountains reflect off the water.*

*Until we meet again, stay well, and God bless.*
*Your friend,*
*Ed*

Somehow, as I read the letter to myself, my heart felt empty and yet whole. When we had said goodbye on Christmas Eve, I sensed that it might be the last I would see of him. Yet, the letter came at what Ed would deem an appropriate time, just as he had planned, right before the board meeting, to give me the extra lift I needed.

"Good morning, gentlemen," I said as I walked confidently into the boardroom. Bill sat at the head of the table, and I took my seat in the first chair to his left. Martin Shafer sat directly across from me. Martin was at least 75, had been CEO of two major orthopedic companies over the last 30 years, and had taken both of them public. Directly to his right, Alyssa Cambridge had been

CFO for a significant, top-five orthopedic company for several years. She had been guiding US Ortho for the last five years. Finally, there were the Sorensen brothers, Jim and Steve. Jim was the head of Sorensen Medical for years, and his younger brother Steve took the helm when Jim stepped down to pursue other ventures. Jim, though 70, was still involved in the medical industry and sought after by many companies. On the other hand, Steve spent more time on the golf course but was still very knowledgeable. At 65, he looked barely a day over 50.

"Thanks to all of you for being here this morning," Bill opened the meeting. "I want to start by talking about the numbers, so I'll turn it over to our VP of Sales, Jack Kaneen."

"Thank you, Bill," I began. "As I'm sure you've all already seen, we finished at 97.6 percent. Unfortunately, we lost accounts early in the year due to factors beyond our control. But I'm happy to report that we clawed our way back through our sales team's diligence and never-give-up attitude. I am extremely proud of my team and am comfortable answering any questions you may have . . ."

"Jack," Alyssa broke in, "we told you at the beginning of the year that we needed 100 percent."

"Yes, I realize that," I replied.

"This board finds anything less than 100 percent unacceptable," Jim Sorensen added.

There was silence in the room. I looked earnestly into the eyes of each board member, trying to read their expressions and, at the same time, gather my thoughts.

Bill started to chuckle.

"Am I missing something, Bill?" I asked. "I really don't see this as funny," I added in a direct but confused tone.

"Jack," Bill said, "I'm laughing because I did something you may not agree with." He looked around the room, and I could see that each board member was aware of whatever he was about to say. "After you communicated the difficulty we had with Maine Medical Center in the early negotiations last year, the board and I agreed to hold back on the quota number by five percent."

"I guess we forgot to tell you," Steve said, grinning.

"Okay," I forced myself to take a deep breath, "what does this mean?"

"It means, Jack, that you and that incredible team of yours actually delivered 103.5 percent to quota!" Martin Shafer exclaimed.

Again, there was silence.

"Jack," Alyssa expounded, "this means that you reached your company bonus and personal bonus, which total over half of your base salary, so you are looking at a $175,000 bonus. In addition, each team member has also maxed out their bonuses."

"I, I don't know what to say," I was still trying to grasp everything they were telling me.

"Jack, there is more," Martin continued, "we have decided to expand our infrastructure and create a new position, President of Sales US.

"Jack," Bill said proudly, "we're asking you to step into that role."

"I'm speechless, Bill."

"Jack, the company believes in you," Jim explained further. "And, as a sign of our faith, we want to offer you this opportunity to advance your career."

"The base salary for this position will be $300,000," Alyssa shared, always the one to focus on numbers. And we're working on the details for a new bonus structure."

"Of course, we will need to backfill your VP of Sales position," Steve added, "but we're sure you will bring us good candidates."

"So, what do you think, Jack?" Bill asked.

"Well, Bill," I measured my words, "first of all, I want to thank each of you for the vote of confidence." Then, I looked again at the faces that now seemed suddenly expectant. Given this year's turbulence, I have also been reassessing. This is a big step, which I'm sure will require the same or more hours. That has never bothered me before, but it affects my family, so we will need to make a decision as a family. I want to talk this over with Mary."

"Jack, that's perfectly fine," Bill responded. "Take a couple days and talk it over. Then, can we regroup here on Friday at the same time?"

"That would be good," I replied. "I also want to reiterate that this has been a team effort. My team should be the ones getting the accolades. They did this. They have a never, ever give up attitude, and it shows."

"Jack," said Martin, who had been mostly quiet up to this point. "You have that something that many people in your position lose sight of."

"What's that?" I asked.

"You never forget where you came from," he said. "You are one of those individuals who has stayed true to yourself. We could use more people like you in this business, Jack."

"Thank you, Martin," I smiled sincerely. "Coming from you, that really means a lot. You are very kind."

"Okay, I think we are done here," Bill said. "Jack, we will see you at 9 a.m. on Friday."

After shaking hands with every board member, I retreated to my office and shut the door. Then, sinking into my chair, I sat in disbelief for a moment or two. Before Bill started laughing, I was sure they would hand me a severance package. But then, it was as if the room had shifted. Everything changed; we made 103.7 percent to quota, maxed out our bonuses, and they created a President of Sales position.

I picked up the phone to call Mary but put it down before it rang. If ever there were a time when I wished I could talk to Ed, this was indeed it. I picked up his letter. Scrolling down with my eyes, I came to the sentence that read, "Today, you will be challenged."

*How could he have known?*

I stood up and walked to the windows. My thoughts stopped and started and changed lanes like the cars on the street below. *How could I turn this offer down? How could I turn my back on the farm and its growing dreams? How could I choose between the two?*

I tried to collect my thoughts but clearly needed more time and space to think.

For the first time in all the years I had worked at US ortho, I decided to go home before my day had even started.

"Kathy?"

"Yes, Jack," Kathy answered on the other end of the receiver.

"Can you intercept my messages, and unless it's important, I'll return all my calls in the morning?"

"Are you feeling okay, Jack?" Kathy asked, sounding concerned. "Did everything go alright at the board meeting?"

"I'm fine, Kathy," I assure her. "Everything went fine. I'm going to go over to the stables for a while and then head home."

There was a pause on the other end, "Do I hear you correctly? Jack Kaneen is . . . playing hooky?"

"Yep," I laughed, "you heard it straight from the horse's mouth."

"You got it, Jack," Kathy chirped. "I got you covered. Enjoy the day. It's actually going to reach 45 degrees."

"I'll take it," I said while shutting down my computer and gathering my coat and bag.

I paused for a second as I walked through the doorway into the hall and looked back at my office. I felt as if a weight had lifted from my shoulders. Then, turning toward the elevator, I found myself whistling "Danny Boy" in honor of Ed.

I called Mary as I pulled from the parking garage onto the highway and pointed the car toward the stables.

The call went to voicemail.

"Hey, Mar, the meeting went well this morning. Nothing to worry about, but I wanted to let you know I'm going to head over to the barn and spend a little time with Dreamer. Then I'm heading home. Kathy joked that I was playing hooky. I just needed some time alone to think and to be present. I'll fill you in when I get home."

Not used to being here on a weekday, I noticed the activity I had never taken the time to see before. Alissa was tacking up one of her younger prospects, and Tucker Winslow, the western trainer, was working with one of his many show horses in the ring.

"Jack!" Alissa exclaimed. "This is a surprise. We never get to see you during the week."

"I know. I'm as surprised as you are," I said as I watched her putting the bridle on a beautiful bay Quarter Horse gelding.

"Are you just here to visit, or are you going to ride?"

"I thought I might try a little trail ride with Dreamer if it's dry enough out there."

"Oh, yeah," Alissa replied, "the warmer days have left the trail behind the stable in great condition. I had one of our horses out there yesterday."

"That's great. I'll get Dreamer and see if she's up for it."

"She'll be fine, Jack. Nothing phases her. As we like to say, she's bomb-proof."

"Okay then," I chuckled, "I'll get her ready."

"Enjoy. The weather forecast said it would be 45 today, but it feels more like 55 with that sun."

Dreamer was in her stall, and she seemed happy to see me. She followed me to the tack stall, and I picked her feet out. Then I brushed her slowly, and I could tell she was enjoying it. I took the time to massage just below her withers which, by the way she extended her neck, must have felt really good. And it wasn't just good for Dreamer; the more I brushed her, the easier and more relaxed my breathing got, and I could feel the morning's tension begin to slip away.

*How do you walk away from an offer like that?*

"It's not about the money, son," I could almost hear Ed's voice as I cinched up Dreamer's girth.

"No, it's not," I said into thin air. *It's about appreciating the simple things that make a difference and being true to myself, isn't it, old friend?*

"Well, girl," I said softly, "life is about decisions. You were a good decision, that's for sure."

As Dreamer and I made our way out of the barn and headed toward the trail, I felt as if I were about to embark on the road less traveled, literally and figuratively. The woods along the trail brought me a deep sense of inner peace and quiet confidence.

When I got home, everyone greeted me at the door: Mary, Patrick, Elizabeth, and even Brady. Before I could even put my bag down, Mary gave me a huge hug.

"You did it, Jack!" she exclaimed. "We're so proud of you!"

"What's all this?"

"Kathy told me your news," Mary explained as I leaned down to pet Brady.

"She did?"

"Sorry to spoil your surprise," Mary said as I hung up my coat, "but I saw that I had missed a call from you, so I called back. I must have been on the phone with Kathy when you left your message that you were going to the stables." She paused before exclaiming again, "Not only did you make your numbers, you totally exceeded their expectations!"

"We did," I nodded. "But, Mary, I think there may be more to what happened at the meeting today than Kathy told you, more than Kathy knows."

I could see the confusion on Mary's face, but just then, the phone rang.

"Hello," Mary answered.

"Who is it?" I asked, mouthing my words.

"It's your sister," Mary mouthed back while grabbing a pen and notepad from the counter.

"Patrick, Elizabeth, why don't we get you bundled up," I suggested. "This 45-degree day makes the snow perfect for building snowmen. Mom and I will be out in a little bit."

"Okay!" they called in unison, heading straight for their winter gear.

Once they were stuffed into their gloves and hats, tied into their boots, and zipped into their coats, they tumbled out the back door with Brady, wagging his tail at top speed.

I came back to where Mary sat holding the phone.

"Yes, okay, I see. That sounds good, but we'll have to run some final numbers."

I didn't have to guess; I knew exactly what they were talking about.

"We won't," Mary assured her. "We'll discuss it and give you a call in the morning."

"Annie?" I confirmed as soon as she hung up.

"Yeah, she thinks we could get the farm for $650,000 before it even hits the market in a week, something about making an offer before it even goes to 'Coming Soon.'"

"Wow!" I exclaimed. "That's much quicker than I expected."

"It is," Mary agreed. "But what's this other news you have?"

"Why don't you fix us both some hot tea while I go change. We can sit outside while the kids play, and I'll tell you all about it."

We had built three snowmen, one for Patrick and one for Elizabeth. Then Elizabeth insisted that we make one for Brady too. Then we took the kids out for pizza at Two Brothers and finished the evening with hot chocolate and marshmallows. It had been a perfect afternoon before they started back to school the next day, but it had also been a long, emotional day for me.

I told Mary about the promotion and the raise. We had talked about it a little while the kids played in the snow, but after I had come back down from putting the kids to bed, we had curled up on the sofa to finish our conversation.

We talked about the pros and cons. We reviewed the numbers again and again: my bonus, the newly offered salary, the price of the farm, the estimated cost of renovations on the farm, and the amount of available cash we could expect from selling our house.

"With a $175,000 bonus," Mary had said, emphasizing those numbers, "buying the farm is definitely doable, Jack."

Those digits had certainly replaced any visions of sugarplums that may have been left over in my mind from Christmas. The irony was that my success in leading the team to finish at 103 percent to quota was what earned me a $175,000 bonus, the offer of a promotion, and a raise. Yet, that same bonus made buying the farm a real possibility. I kept thinking I would be crazy to turn down the promotion I'd just been offered. Still, in the next breath, I would think I would be crazy to turn down the opportunity to bring the farm back into our family.

The house was quiet, all except for Brady snoring at my side. Mary and I both seemed to be lost in our thoughts.

Finally, I reached for Mary's hand. "Mary, what do you really think we should do?"

"Jack, the money isn't the deciding factor here. It's about doing what makes you happy."

"But what about you?" I asked. "It can't be all about me. What about the kids?"

"I wouldn't have pursued the idea of buying the farm if I didn't think it could be positive for our family. But I think as long as we are together as a family, I would live in a one-room apartment and make that work." Her sensitive, blue eyes looked right into mine. "Annie would say, 'Listen to your heart, and your dreams will follow,' right? So, what does your heart tell you?"

"Now you sound like Ed."

"The janitor again?" Mary asked.

"Yes," I paused. "Ed's gone."

"Gone?" Mary asked with surprise, clearly caught a little off guard.

"He didn't die or anything," I assured her, "at least not that I know of. He left. I thought that might be the case when we said goodbye on Christmas Eve. I got a letter from him before I went into the boardroom." I reached into my pocket and pulled out his letter. "He knew," I said as I handed it to Mary. "Somehow, he knew what would happen in the board meeting today."

After looking it over for a minute, she returned it to me and said, "He knew your value, Jack. And he knew the company would value you that much in the end too. But, he also knew that their offer would tempt you and challenge your sense of purpose."

"I'll say," I shook my head.

"It's almost like he is here with you at this crossroad."

"You know, you're right, Mary," I said. "He's taught me a lot, and what he has taught me will help me make the right decision for our family."

"Why don't we sleep on it?" Mary suggested.

"You're right again," I sighed. "If we get a good night's sleep, I think we'll have our answer in the morning."

Mary stood up and stretched, ready to head upstairs.

"I'll be up there in just a few minutes," I said.

"Okay," she leaned down to kiss me on the cheek, "just don't be too late. The sleep will do you a world of good."

As she headed upstairs, I reopened the letter that I still held in my hand and read it one more time.

~

# CHAPTER TWENTY

# MAKING DREAMS COME TRUE

C OME ON," HE YELLED, "THE FISHING WILL BE excellent this morning. I can feel it in my old bones."

As I approached the dock, he said, "It's just as calm but not as cool as last time."

With that, I untied the bow and hopped in while he untied the stern and threw the motor into reverse. We backed around, then we raced down to Arnold's Point. It was a beautiful morning, and the lake was again like a mirror. Two loons followed along low across the water, almost as if they were watching over us before settling into their fishing grounds.

"Loons have always amazed me," I replied as the motor came down to trolling speed.

"What amazes you about them, Jack?"

"Well, they stick together, watch over their babies, and it just seems like they don't have a care in the world. They are just part of this place."

"You know, they mate for life and are all about family," he said. "Might say for them, it's the simple things that have made all the difference."

"Hand me your line and let's sew a real winner on for you this time," he said with a grin nestled beneath his white beard.

He reminded me to go a little deeper today as we dropped the lines because the water temperature was slightly warmer.

"So, you've learned a little since the last time we were out here."

"I have?" I asked. "What do you think I've learned?"

"You're present, son. You've learned to be present. How often have you seen those loons and never thought twice about them?"

"That's a good point," I conceded.

"You see, Jack," he went on as the lines caught some tension against the slow trolling speed of the motor, "when you are present, you notice things. You see the world around you uninhibited by stress, allowing you to be true to yourself."

"I guess I never thought about it that way."

"Son, the sad part about it is that so many people never get to the point of being present, uninhibited like they were when they were born. You see, when you get there, you find your purpose. And *you*, Jack, have found your purpose! Don't ever lose sight of it," his voice seemed to echo off the mountains, amplified as it bounced across the valley.

"Hey! You have a strike!" he said, "Let's bring 'em in. You got this, Jack, you got this . . . you got this . . . you got this . . ."

I sat on the edge of the bed in the quiet dawn. Looking back over my shoulder, I could see Mary sleeping peacefully. *At least I didn't wake her up this time,* I thought to myself.

Quietly, I made my way downstairs with Brady by my side. I fed him and put on a fresh pot of coffee. When it was ready, I poured a cup and sat on the sofa. Brady didn't waste any time resting his head on my lap.

"Well, ol' boy," I said. "It's time, isn't it?"

I almost expected him to answer, and, in his own way, he was giving me his answer.

"You're going to be right by my side, aren't you, boy?"

I could hear Mary in the kitchen pouring herself a cup of coffee. When she sat next to me, she didn't even have to ask me about my decision. She knew. And I knew that she agreed.

"Amazing what a good night's sleep will do for you, Jack?"

"That definitely helped," I agreed. "And you were right about Ed being with me at this crossroads . . . and, like Robert Frost, he's telling me to take the road less traveled because it will make all the difference."

"Very insightful man, this janitor," Mary mused.

"I wish you could have met him."

"So, when are you going to tell them?"

"Monday," I replied. "I'll tell them Monday. I have decided to recommend Carol for my position."

"You have spoken highly of her, Jack. Do you think she is ready?"

"She is, and, besides, I intend to let Bill and the board know I will be available to consult over the next year. There will be a lot to do in the coming weeks, but I must ensure I leave the company prepared. It's important whether it's Carol or someone else that they are set up for success."

"I'm proud of you, Jack," Mary added in her wonderful caring tone.

"Thank you, Mary, thanks to you and my conniving sister," I added in jest, "for prodding me along to the point where it made it plain to see."

"That's what family does, right?" she said. "We watch out for each other."

"Yeah," I laughed slightly, "just like the loon family at the lake, always sticking together and taking care of each other."

"What made you think of that?" Mary asked.

"Let's just say I'm noticing more than I used to since I've learned to be present," I smiled. "That's true," Mary agreed. "So, what do you say, we give that 'conniving sister' of yours a call?"

"GOOD morning," I said as I sat at the conference table.

With everyone seated, Bill began, "Jack . . ."

"Bill, before we get too far into this, may I have a minute to address the board?" I had never interrupted Bill while speaking to a group, but he had already assumed I was taking the position, and I felt certain the board also believed that.

"Sure, Jack," Bill said, taking a seat. "You have the floor."

All eyes were on me.

"I can't tell you all how honored I am that you have created this new position for me," I began. "It shows your faith in me and my team and our value to the company. I have just completed my eighth year with this company, and US Ortho has been good to my family and me. We have tackled what many in this industry would see as insurmountable odds. We have not only proved them wrong, but we have exceeded all of their expectations. I didn't accomplish that alone but with my team and your support, who believed we could do it yearly. We set goals many would say were lofty. Some might say too lofty; however, they did not prove too high for us. We believed in ourselves, our team, and our strategy. Every year, we execute our approach at the corporate level. Our team implemented the tactical plan that gave us the new business to reach our needed numbers.

"This company, these people, have been my life. I appreciate your faith in me, but I must also inform you that I cannot accept the position you graciously offered me."

The silence in the room momentarily left me feeling as if the oxygen had disappeared, not just the sound. My heart began to race, and I felt sure they could hear it, but I knew I was doing the right thing.

"Jack," Bill broke the silence, "we weren't expecting this." I could tell that he was trying to put the pieces together in his head.

"Bill, I know this is a big shock, but I assure you that wasn't my intent."

"I know we told you to take a few days to think over our offer," Jim Sorensen said, "but are you sure you are making the right decision here?"

"Jack," Alyssa continued, "we have worked through your compensation and bonus, and if you hit your number this year, you will bring home over $500,000. Is that really a number you are prepared to walk away from?"

"Trust me, Alyssa," I assured her, "Mary and I have run the numbers, but that's just not what I am looking for right now."

"Jack, I'm not sure what more we can do, but is there any way we can entice you to stay?" Martin asked in earnest.

"No, Martin, your offer is more than gracious, and the compensation package is certainly tempting; but I have grown and changed over the . . ."

"Jack," Bill interrupted, "you have an airtight non-compete agreement, and you will have to sit out for 18 months no matter where you go."

"Bill, I apologize if I have given you the wrong impression. I wouldn't think of going to any other company after my experience growing the team with US Ortho. Mary and I have decided to buy our old family farm in Maine."

"Jack, that sounds wonderful," Steve piped in, "but you are nowhere near retirement age."

"Oh, you're right about that, Steve," I said. "In fact, I really believe that I am making a move to a career from which I will never want to retire."

"A farmer?" Bill asked, and I could hear the disappointment tinged with anger in his voice. "Jack, no offense, but you have way too much experience with management to throw that all away."

"I agree wholeheartedly, Bill," I assured him. "My experience here has been invaluable. And while my work in orthopedics is done, I am hoping that my work with business leaders is not. We are not only going to breed show horses and train horses and riders, but I will also start a business to work with managers and team members to increase their leadership skills and help teams function at their highest levels."

"You can do that with *horses?*" Alyssa asked.

"It's called equine-assisted learning, "I explained. "It's not widely known in the business community, but I assure you it will be."

"What is your time frame, Jack?" Martin asked. "We need a replacement for you as soon as possible as we're already into the new year. And, although we will have to discuss it as a board, I don't believe we will be offering the position we created for you to anyone else."

"I have a replacement in mind, and I know you will be happy with her."

"Her?" Alyssa looked pleasantly surprised.

"I am recommending that Carol Anderson assume my position," I began. "I have mentored Carol over the last few years, and she is up to the task. She is responsible for getting the Maine Med account back for us. She has consistently grown her business and developed new relationships every year. Her peers also respect her and go to her often with sales questions."

"Jack, I'm sure I speak for the board," Jim said, "when I say that we wish you would reconsider."

"I appreciate that Jim and the faith the board has put in me. I am more than willing to stay as a consultant to ensure a smooth transition. By appointing Carol to my position, I think you will do what's best for the company since she will hit the ground running."

"Jack," Bill said, "I won't say that I'm not disappointed. We were all really counting on you. However, if you believe that Carol is the person for the job, I trust your recommendation. You have put your heart and soul into this company, and I want to acknowledge that."

"Thank you, Bill," I said, feeling emotion well inside, "you can't know how much I appreciate that."

"Okay," Bill continued, addressing the board, "We need to take a vote. All in favor of Jack's recommendation for our new Vice President of Sales?"

The board responded with all ayes, although Martin wanted to make sure I stayed on as a consultant, even if only remotely, at least through the year. I agreed, and with that, the meeting adjourned. The next quarter of an hour was filled with lots of handshaking, expressions of gratitude, and some questions about the farm and equine-assisted learning. I knew my decision was not what the board expected, but it was nice to know that the board members respected my reasons for leaving. As I walked out of the board room, I could almost feel a door closing as another was beginning to open.

Once I could retreat to my office, I rang Kathy.

"Kathy," I said, "I need you to call Carol and see if she can come in tomorrow morning for a meeting with me."

"Sure," Kathy replied before pausing. "Jack, is everything okay? It seems a little out of the ordinary," she added with concern.

"Everything is great, Kathy, all good," I assured her. "Just tell her there are some issues I need to discuss with her going into the new year, and I want her thoughts on future strategy."

"Got it," Kathy replied, although I could tell she still wasn't buying into what I was saying.

"Kathy," I added, "make sure she knows she has no reason to worry."

TUESDAY morning, when I got off the elevator, Carol was chatting with Kathy over a cup of Dunkin' at her desk.

"Good morning, ladies," I called enthusiastically. "Carol, give me just a minute to fire up my computer. You have time to freshen up that coffee."

"Great, Jack," she said as she headed toward the break room. "I'll be right there."

"So, what's going on, Jack?" Carol asked as she entered the office.

"Shut the door if you don't mind, Carol. It's all good."

"Well, that's a relief," Carol said as she took a sip of her coffee. "But I must admit, you sure do have me curious."

"What I'm about to tell you is confidential," I began.

"Okay," Carol seemed even more perplexed.

"I have decided to resign as VP of Sales for US Ortho."

I could hear Carol swallow her last sip of coffee in the silence.

"Are you serious, Jack?" she asked. "What happened? Was 97 percent not good enough for them? You let me know what you need, Jack, because I'll tell the board all the work that went into last year and what a great leader you are . . ."

"Carol, Carol," I cut her short. "Let me explain. First off, we didn't make 97 percent to quota."

"We didn't?" she asked, looking shocked. "Was it that bad?"

"No, we didn't," I paused, feeling a little like I was tricking her the way Bill had tricked us. "Thanks to you and the team's effort, we made 103 percent to quota."

"That's not possible," Carol responded quickly.

"It's not," I concurred, "except that during the Maine Med bid early last year, Bill convinced the board to drop the number. He conveniently didn't tell me, so I could never tell you or the team."

"So, what does this all mean? Why would you be leaving?"

"I accomplished everything I wanted to and needed to here, and it's time to move on. I have an opportunity to buy my old family farm in Maine, and I'm going to start a horse program, equine-assisted learning, for businesses and teams. I'm going to train and show horses with my family. I'm going to start a sales and leadership consulting business. Who knows, I may even write a book someday?"

"Wow, Jack!" Carol responded with a sense of bewilderment. "Talk about a complete change of direction."

"It might seem like it at first, but it really isn't when you think about it," I explained. "I have realized that it's all about the journey, not the destination. What you do along the way allows us to make a difference. The way I look at this is that everything that I have done in my life up to this point has prepared me to take the next step, to write a new chapter. My mom used to say anything you learn is not lost. I intend to use everything I have learned along the way to help leaders bring out the best in their teams and help them function at their highest level by being more present."

"It sounds like you have really put a lot of thought into this decision," she conceded. "But where does that leave our team? Who will they bring in to replace you?"

"I'm looking at her."

"Me?" Carol asked in disbelief.

"Yes, you," I confirmed. "I have recommended you to replace

me, and the board has unanimously approved the recommendation."

"Jack, are you sure I'm the person for the job?"

"You're ready for it, Carol," I assured her. "I believe in you."

"Jack, I don't know what to say."

"You could start by saying, 'I'll consider it,'" I grinned. "But before you say anything, I want you to think this over. There is a lot that goes with this job. No doubt the salary and bonuses are great, and we can get into that, but it's a lot of responsibility; and, more than that, a lot of sacrifice goes along with it. Sometimes you will need to make decisions that aren't popular, and, as you know, when it comes to numbers, the pressure is always there. There are sometimes long days, and people above and below you will come to you for answers. Now, If I haven't sufficiently scared you, are you interested?"

"Yes!" Carol exclaimed. "I am definitely interested, Jack. I just didn't expect it. I would like to talk this over with David, of course. I'm sure it will mean relocating here to Philly. I suppose remote is a possibility, but this is where everything happens. I know you need to have your finger on the pulse of the business."

"It's a big decision," I agreed. "How do you think David will feel about it?"

"David will be happy for me and never hold me back. He really understands me," Carol smiled. "The good thing is that he can work from anywhere in his job, and, with all his travel, Philly is a great airport to fly from. Even so, I need to discuss it with him because if I accept the position, I must know we are both on board."

"That's smart, Carol. I applaud you for your thought process. Including David in this from the beginning will only strengthen your relationship."

"How soon do you need an answer from me, Jack?"

"I don't want to rush you, Carol," I said, "but I know the

board is anxious to move forward. How about if you plan to let me know on Friday morning?"

"Okay, Jack, I can do that. I was leaning toward saying yes when you first told me, but taking a step back and talking it over with David will help me put it in perspective."

"Actually, if you would like, and if David is available to come down and join you, why don't the two of you stay in town and explore the city a bit more."

"That would be perfect, Jack. I will have an answer for you on Friday morning. I'm not sure if it will be the answer you want, but I can't tell you how much I appreciate this and how much your faith in me means."

I don't think Carol knew whether to shake my hand or give me a hug when we stood to end the meeting, but she opted for a heartfelt hug.

CAROL was punctual as usual on Friday morning, arriving with coffee in hand.

"I hope your early arrival is an omen of good news," I said as I greeted her.

"Kathy, hold my calls, will you?" I said as I passed by her desk.

"Consider it done, Jack. I'll take messages."

"Great, come on down, Carol." She followed me into my office and shut the door for the second time this week.

"Jack, this is a really tough decision. David and I had a couple of great discussions, and there are

a lot of positives, but there are a few negatives too. Some of the negatives are related, quite frankly, to the stress I have seen you under. I also know the kind of hours you put in. I called you at 7 p.m. many evenings, and I believe that's taxing on a family and a relationship."

"It is, Carol. There is no doubt about it," I said, folding my hands on my desk and leaning into the conversation. "Success comes at a price. For some, it's too high a price. But, the people who aren't afraid of the climb and the landmines along the way often do well and find what they are looking for. Carol, let's face it, you hire people you believe to have goals and want to succeed. While we haven't always agreed, you have always put the company and the team first. You will be a great leader if this is what you choose."

"Thank you, Jack. That means a lot to me coming from you. Your faith in me has played a big role in this decision," she smiled, "and that's why I am honored to accept this position."

"That's wonderful, Carol! As I said, I know you will be a great leader for this company. I just want you to know that even though I won't be here day in and day out, you can always call me. We all need advocates who we can trust to give it to us straight. I can tell you from experience that you will need that in this position. There will be times when you, and only you, can make a decision, and that's when leadership can feel lonely. You can't do this like I have done until recently."

"What do you mean by that?"

"I mean, you can't work 24-7 like you alluded that I was doing," I said, only partly in jest. "You were right about the stress you have seen weighing me down, but, through the last part of this year, I have been able to find the balance I was missing. Leadership will certainly challenge your life's balance; if you don't have balance, you may appear to shine in your position. But your personal, spiritual, and family life will all pay the price, and that will eventually affect your overall performance. The weariness of it can get the best of you if you let it. Use it as a barometer to know when the scales are tipping out of balance. It seems like you and David have a strong relationship. Just keep communicating openly, and allow him and your other advocates to offer you a reality check when you need it. Just remember that it's the simple things that make the difference, be true to who you are, and always follow your heart, and you will do just fine, Carol."

"That's great advice, as always, Jack. You have been an important mentor to me, and I will strive to live up to the faith you've shown in me."

"I'll be your advocate, Carol. Just call me when you need me."

"I can't tell you how much I appreciate that Jack, and I will be picking up the phone to call you often. You can count on it."

"I asked Bill to call a board meeting this morning, hoping you would accept the position. The board is anxious to start this new season with you. We have about 15 minutes before the meeting starts, so why don't you take some time and refill that coffee while I have a little chat with Kathy about all the changes."

As Carol headed to the break room, I asked Kathy to come in. She already knew something was up after having scheduled two private meetings with Carol in one week. When I asked her to close the door as I had done with Carol, I could see her eyes widen. Assuring her she had nothing to worry about, I explained what had occurred in the board meeting on Monday and in my two meetings with Carol.

"Jack," Kathy said with tears welling in her eyes, "I'm surprised you're stepping away, but I'm not surprised that Carol is taking your place. No one will ever replace you, but she will do a good job."

"People come and go," I said, "but the mark of a great organization is that it transcends individuals. The company should continue to thrive if a leader has done a good job. I think we have built that culture here."

"I'll miss you dearly, Jack. We all will," Kathy said with heartfelt emotion. "You have meant so much to this company."

"Kathy, I really appreciate it. I will miss you, too, but the good news is that I will stay on as a consultant through the end of the year to help with the transition."

"I hope they know what they are losing." Kathy gave me a big hug, turned quickly to hide the tears, and headed back to her office.

I spent the rest of the morning in the board meeting, talking to people in the office like Chad and calling individual team members to let them know the news firsthand. It was a shock to everyone, which was understandable, but we all got through it.

When I shut down my computer that afternoon, I longed to hear the whistle of "Danny Boy." I walked to the windows like so many times before. Some of those times, I had stared outside, but I had really been thinking about what I needed to get done. I was thankful that I had learned the art of being present and practiced it more and more often. Like the windshield analogy, I was looking forward with great wonder and aspirations toward what was next.

# CHAPTER TWENTY-ONE

~

# GONE FISHING

EVERY DAY WAS FILLED WITH WORK, THE KIND OF work that made you tired but allowed you to sleep like a baby. I continued to work with the horses daily. I used the round pen we had situated between the new barn and the upper pasture every day to work with the equine education horses at liberty. Brady would sit outside the enclosure near the gate, watching our every move. He was so patient.

Dreamer was perfect for the job. It would only take her about 10 minutes before she would turn her ears toward me and begin to lick her lips. Sage was a willing participant as well. Bob and Noreen gave us their horses, Sonny and Nancy, so we could keep them on the farm. And given that they were each about 15 years old, they fit right into the equine program and Annie's lessons. They had slightly different ways of expressing themselves, yet I could tell they enjoyed the work and the attention. I loved standing in the center as one of the horses traveled around the pen. Sometimes they would snort at me when they first got going, protesting the realization that we had to do some work. Sometimes they would even kick out their hind legs in a mild buck. It was their way of giving off energy.

On one occasion, Sonny refused to leave my side. Instead, he followed me around the pen as I picked up my lunge whip. Every time I made a move, he quietly followed like he had been seeking leadership for some time and now had another person besides Bob he could trust. Sonny was a 15-year-old black Quarter Horse who stood just over 15 hands and had a very developed neck and shoulders, almost like an old-style Morgan. Bob said he had been shown in the halter classes when he was younger and had won several championships. He knew he was a champion, and I loved watching him. I hadn't figured out if he was inviting me into his little herd. Still, it was clear that we had developed a relationship, a partnership that would last a lifetime.

All of this work was an exercise in building trust. Horses don't communicate like dogs or cats. They are intuitive, and their body movements tell you almost everything you need to know. That's why they are such good coaches. They seek leadership, and I believe they would do most anything for you if they trust you. Some would think I'm crazy, but I would do almost anything for them.

IT was a hot day in July, just after the fourth. I was out bailing hay, getting as much possible for the winter to cut costs when I felt my phone vibrate in my pocket. It was a welcome break, and I was excited to see the call from Carol.

I had continued to have weekly calls with her, and occasionally Bill would join in. The consulting checks were a nice added benefit, but mostly it was good to keep the connections. Carol was doing a fabulous job, tracking ahead of their numbers through the year's first half. I couldn't have been happier for her.

"Ready to come back yet?" she joked.

"Not a chance," I laughed, "not a chance. I'm having too much fun working."

"Fun working?" Carol repeated my words, "Now that's a new one on me."

"So, how's business going?"

"Well, that's why I'm calling," she said. "Are you ready to go with your equine program?"

"Yeah, we're ready," I felt a sense of pride to confirm. "In fact, I just completed my certification for equine-assisted education, and we have some bookings starting in August. Why do you ask?"

"'Are you ready for this, Jack?" Carol paused for dramatic effect. "I want to bring the team up for two days of your training. Bill already approved it."

"That's great!" I exclaimed. "But I have to admit, I'm shocked! How did you convince Bill and the board to go along with that?"

"Well, I told them our leadership consultant said balance was crucial, so I built it into the budget." Carol laughed.

"That it is, that it is," I laughed along with her. "You're a good student!"

"Well, I learned from the best," Carol said.

"Tell you what, I'll send you the proposal breakdown and the agenda for the two-day conference, and let's reconnect next week to discuss the details."

"Perfect," Carol replied, "always good talking with you, Jack."

"Great talking with you too."

I dropped the phone back into my pocket with a big smile. As I returned to work, I couldn't help but wonder how so much had fallen into place over the past six months.

Carol obviously had to find a home in Philly, and, after we had invited her to take a look at our house, she and David thought it would be perfect for them. So they didn't have to endure house-hunting all over the city, and we never even had to put our house on the market. And, because of that blessing, we had been able to put an offer on the farm before it even went on the market.

The following months had been busy, but each day ended with a sense of accomplishment.

As we anticipated, the farm needed a lot of work. Some of the old posts and beams of the barn that sat in the field directly across from the house were not in the best shape, but fortunately, Annie and Mary had done a great job accounting for the construction costs. We had finished the indoor arena the last week of May, and it looked amazing.

By June, we had been up and running. We joked about the famous line from the Kevin Costner movie *Field of Dreams*, "If you build it, they will come." But the truth was that we had filled the stalls with 12 local boarder horses almost as soon as we opened for business.

We had also just finished adding four small, rustic bunk houses around the edge of the north pasture. We already had plans to use them for guests who were either part of the equine learning program, overnight riding clinics, or for people who wanted a leisurely dude ranch vacation to do some trail riding.

In addition to the boarder's horses, we brought in six older geldings for equine-assisted learning, and we added two beautiful Quarter Horse mares who were about to foal anytime. One of those foals would undoubtedly be named Discerning Destiny, Destiny for short.

Annie was almost at the max with students, so much so that Mary started helping with the beginner children. I could see the look of fulfillment in her and how much she loved it. It wasn't just that she loved the lessons. Her joy came from the fact that we were doing all of this as a family. It felt like we were living a dream, and we joked that we had to pinch ourselves to ensure it was all real.

I looked up to wipe the sweat from my brow. As if they had

known I was thinking about them, Mary was walking toward the field with a tall glass of icy lemonade in each hand. Annie followed behind her with her own glass, pointing with her free hand toward the big pine tree.

That tree had survived the years since our family last had the farm, and we often took breaks in its shade, revisiting our memories as we sipped on something cool to drink.

"Ladies, I must say I'm glad . . . no, I'm thankful," I corrected myself, "for the nudge to follow my dreams. It's making a huge difference in my life."

"Ours too," Mary and Annie said almost simultaneously.

"We're a pretty good team, don't you think?" said Annie, holding up her glass of lemonade for a toast.

"I would agree, I would agree," I replied. "And your lemonade isn't bad either," I said, clinking my glass with Annie's and Mary's and taking another sip.

"Jack," Mary said, "I advertised online for another part-time trainer and someone willing to help in the barn. But what do you think about making up some fliers around town? I think Maggie would let us put some in the window at her diner?"

"'Sure," I replied. "I think that's a great idea. I'm heading to the grain store in the morning, so I can put one up there, and I'll stop by Maggie's."

"Great!" Annie exclaimed. "We could use the help . . . like yesterday."

"I'll get the flier made up before I throw the steaks on the grill," Mary said

THE following day, after the stalls were done and the horses turned out, I made my run into town armed with Mary's fliers. The flier read:

*Wanted:*
*Part-Time Trainer and Assistant Barn Manager*
*Kaneen Stables*
*Please inquire in person or by calling (207) 474-3877*

Maggie was so friendly. She kept a couple of fliers by the register, allowed me to put one on each side of the front door in the windows, and sent me off with a fresh cup of coffee and one of her famous apple turnovers. It didn't last even half the eight-mile drive back to the farm.

ONE day, I worked with Dreamer in the round pen as I often did. Curiously, she stopped and turned her ears up toward the driveway and the house. Then, she started moving again, repeating what she had just done.

"Come on, girl," I encouraged, "there is nothing over there."

Finally, she started licking her lips, and with a gentle command of woah, I asked her to stop. She stood there, still and silent, so I simply turned a quarter turn away from her and just waited. Then I could see why she had stopped and started. Mary was standing off in the distance by the house with someone motioning down toward us, but I couldn't determine who it was.

I was still trying to get Dreamer to follow me around the round pen as Mary walked toward us with who I hoped was a job applicant. As they approached, I stood as still as Dreamer, thinking I was looking at a ghost.

"Ed?" his name caught in my throat as I walked toward him. "Is that really you?" I could feel tears stinging my eyes.

Mary just stood there, not knowing what exactly was happening. Then, suddenly, her eyes lit up. "It's you, isn't it? You're the janitor!" she exclaimed.

"Yes, ma'am, that would be me," he said, tucking his thumbs into his black suspenders. "I've been called by many titles, but you can call me Ed."

"Of course, Ed," she beamed. "It's such a pleasure to finally meet you. I must say, you have made quite an impact on Jack, on our whole family."

"It's a pleasure to meet you too, Mary," he reached to shake her hand. "And this," he said as he waved his arm outward across the pasture and then looked straight into my eyes, "this is a piece of heaven, isn't it?"

"It really is," I agreed, still staring in disbelief.

"Well," Mary said, "I'm going to leave you two to catch up." She turned toward the house but quickly turned back. "By the way, Ed, we have an extra room, and you are welcome to stay as long as you'd like."

"Thank you, ma'am," Ed nodded again.

Dreamer stood there by my shoulder, as relaxed as she ever was. Then she quietly walked right up to the edge of the fence by Ed.

"Good girl," Ed said. "What a beautiful girl!"

"Ed," I said as I followed her to the fence, "this is Dreamer."

"She is named appropriately, Jack. She's beautiful." Like a reflex, Ed placed the backside of his hand through the fence to not make Dreamer think he had a treat but allowed her to smell his hand and decide for herself if he passed the test. It was pretty evident that he did because Dreamer just stood there, made a big sigh, and allowed Ed to gently stroke her neck through the fence.

"Jack, can we take a walk?"

Without saying a word, I put Dreamer's halter on, and we walked down the dirt road along the north side of the pasture. Brady just followed quietly by my side.

"I knew this was your calling from the moment you mentioned it, and I can see now that this place is a part of you. It was before and will be forever. You're going to use this place to fulfill the purpose you told me about, and you will touch more lives and open more hearts and minds than you could ever have dreamed of back in Philly."

"Discerning Destiny," I said softly.

"You see, Jack, you didn't need a visit from Dickens' three ghosts to bring you a message. You just had to ask yourself the right questions. Then all you had to do was listen to your heart," Ed placed his hand on his heart and, with a twinkle in his eye, said, "and your dreams were never far behind."

"Ed, I don't know why you came into my life or why you're here now, but I hope every angel wears suspenders and mops floors. Everyone needs a janitor."

"Jack, everyone needs people in their life that care. You have all these people around you who were always here for you. It's just that you weren't present enough to see them. Dreamer here, she is always present, and she will keep you grounded. She will let you know when you start off the rails. As for me, janitor, cabby, ironworker, counselor, I've had a lot of different assignments; but I came to apply for this one." He pulled Mary's flier out of his pocket and held it up.

"What do you mean?" I asked, still having difficulty believing Ed was walking beside me.

"The barn help and training job. I don't know if I ever told you, but I spent time around horses when I was younger too. So, what do you say? Are you willing to give an old man a chance to prove himself?"

"Ed, you don't have to prove anything to anyone."

"So, I got the job?"

"It's yours if you want it, and, like Mary said, if you need a place, we have that extra room."

"Well, I should make it clear that if I'm hanging around, I will make sure everyone takes time to recharge their batteries. We all need that balance in life, right?"

"We take at least one day every week, Ed, but I have no doubt you will keep us balanced."

"You go fishing, Jack?"

"Of course," I said as we began to walk back toward the barn.

"Great, then let's go on Saturday morning," he said with a grin peeping out through the cover of his white beard. "I know just how to tie bait on."

"I have no doubt you do," I thought about my dreams of fishing with him. "So, how long do you think you're here for, Ed?"

"I'm here for as long as you need me, Jack," he patted me on the shoulder, "as long as you need me." We both smiled.

"Come on, Brady boy, let's get Dreamer some grain and go up to the house. We have family for dinner."

# ABOUT THE AUTHOR

G ERRY SAVAGE BEGAN A CAREER IN BUSINESS over three decades ago in 1985 after serving on active duty in the United States Marines. In 1991 he entered the field of total joint replacement, winning five President Club awards with Zimmer Orthopedics between 1995 and 2003. Gerry went on to become a distributor for Biomet Orthopedics and then eventually served as a Regional Director for Conformis and Eastern Regional Vice President for MicroPort Orthopedics, Vice President of Sales for Maxx Orthopedics, Senior Vice President of Sales for ALM Orthopedics, and VP of Custom implants and interim COO for NextStep Arthropedix.

Gerry received both his undergraduate and graduate degrees in business administration from Eastern University in St. Davids, Pennsylvania, where he was also an adjunct professor. He is pursuing a Ph.D. in Leadership Philosophy at Lancaster Bible College in Lancaster, PA. In 2018 Gerry Founded The Four Pillars Consulting Group LLC, which provides sales and Leadership training based on his successful book The four Pillars of Sales.

In 2020 Gerry was certified as an Equine Assisted Educator Through The Horse Dreams Program and Alyssa Aubrey at Medicine Horse Ranch in Northern California. This unique program, combined with his business knowledge and knowledge of horses, gives business leaders and teams an out-of-the-classroom experience that will last a lifetime.

An avid equestrian, Gerry's grandfather and father inspired his love for horses. He has competed in the hunter ring over fences as an equestrian throughout central Pennsylvania, where he has lived with his family for the last seventeen years.

When not traveling and working with business leaders and teams throughout the country, Gerry can be found working on his next manuscript, spending time in Maine with family and friends, or at the barn riding horses.

*https://www.fourpillarsconsultinggroup.com/*

*info@fourpillarsconsultinggroup.com*

www.ingramcontent.com/pod-product-compliance
Lightning Source LLC
Chambersburg PA
CBHW061502030726
47503CB00005B/1775